Nosy Neighbor

"Tsk,tsk," he taunted as he stood up, "and losing your temper with me won't solve your problems. Come out of your ivory tower, Hilary, before it's too late, before you really turn into the arrogant bitch that at the moment you're only emulating." With a mocking smile for her look of speechless outrage, he wandered out.

In sudden determination to have the last word, she chased after him. Flinging open the front door, she yelled to his retreating back, "I am not arrogant! And, even if I am, it has nothing whatever to do with you!"

EMMA RICHMOND says she's amiable, undomesticated and an incurable romantic. And, she adds, she has a very forbearing husband, three daughters and a dog of uncertain breed. They live in Kent. A great variety of jobs filled her earlier working years, and more recently she'd been secretary to the chairman of a group of companies. Now she devotes her entire day to writing, although she hasn't yet dispelled her family's illusions that she's reverting to the role of housekeeper and cook! Emma finds writing obsessive, time-consuming—and totally necessary to her well-being.

Books by Emma Richmond

EMMA RICHMOND

A Stranger's Trust

Harlequin Books

TORONTO • NEW YORK • LONDON
AMSTERDAM • PARIS • SYDNEY • HAMBURG
STOCKHOLM • ATHENS • TOKYO • MILAN
MADRID • WARSAW • BUDAPEST • AUCKLAND

Harlequin Presents first edition August 1993
ISBN 0-373-11582-2

Original hardcover edition published in 1991
by Mills & Boon Limited

A STRANGER'S TRUST

CHAPTER ONE

'Good morning.'

'Good morning,' she answered grudgingly as she hastily unpegged her washing and flung it into the laundry basket at her feet.

'Going to rain, do you think?'

Don't answer, she adjured herself; it isn't mandatory; he's only doing it to annoy you—then found she was totally incapable of being as rude as she wanted to be. 'Quite possibly,' she muttered. Her back still turned to him, she picked up the white plastic basket and began to hastily retrace her steps towards the cottage—and she heard him laugh. Swinging round, she glared at him, then promptly averted her gaze as warm grey eyes smiled at her. Her mouth tight, she hurried into the cottage and slammed the door, but that one brief glance had been more than enough for her to take in the fact that he'd removed his shirt as though quite impervious to the chill wind that made everyone else shiver, and was digging over the colonel's vegetable patch with an economy of movement that she might have admired if it had been anyone else but him. Every time she put her nose out of the door, there he seemed to be, and if he wasn't outside he was inside, making provocative

remarks that were guaranteed to drive her into
a fury. She couldn't even ignore him, which
would have been the sensible thing to do; every
time he spoke she found herself lashing back.

And why hadn't the colonel told her he was
renting his house out, she wondered wrath-
fully? Surely that would have been only
common courtesy? Only what courtesy had she
ever given him? she wondered miserably. Or
anyone else for that matter? Dumping her basket
on the floor beside the ironing-board, she felt
her eyes flood with tears.

'That won't help,' a voice said gently as the
back door slowly opened, and she flung up her
head in shock.

'I wasn't, didn't. . . Oh, why don't you go
and put your shirt on?' she exclaimed in
confusion.

'I'm sorry, I didn't stop to think. . . Does it
bother you?'

'No!' But it did. It was such a tough, warm-
looking body. Tanned and fit and healthy, and
he wasn't in the least sorry, she thought irritably. 'And stop smiling at me like that!' she
ordered crossly. 'You wander in and out of my
cottage as though you own the damned place!
Why can't you knock like everyone else?'

'Want me to go out again?' he asked softly.

'No, I don't want you to go out again!'

'Oh, good.' Slipping inside, a look of idiotic
contrition on his strong face, he gave a slow
smile.

'I hate you,' she muttered. He looked ridiculous! His dark hair was ruffled and untidy, and was far too long; and he was too big, too everything, and that antipodean accent grated very severely on nerves already rubbed raw. With a helpless sigh she stared into deep grey eyes that seemed to see too much. Eyes that turned her insides to jelly, scrambled her mind, made her feel dumb and stupid and childish. And every time he came anywhere near her he seemed to generate a sort of static electricity that left her feeling angry and confused. And he must have known that she found his touch distasteful, yet did that stop him? No, it didn't; he still persisted in either standing too close or laying his hand on her arm then watching with amusement as she wrenched herself free. Yet how on earth could one man make her feel so threatened? It was ridiculous and irrational.

'But it isn't only me, is it?' he asked gently. 'You seem to hate everyone, and don't you think this pursuing your career as Miss Efficiency is making you forget you belong to the human race?'

'Don't be silly; you know nothing about my career, pursued or otherwise, and I wish you'd go away,' she added peevishly as she finally managed to drag her eyes from the grey warmth of his. 'I have ironing to do.' Ducking behind the ironing-board, unexpectedly hurt by his observation, she quickly plugged in the iron.

Was she in danger of forgetting who she was?

she wondered bleakly. She was honest enough to admit that she had become very single-minded, but Miss Efficiency? Was that how people saw her? It didn't seem very likely, and she frowned as she tried to view herself objectively. She had an ordinary sort of face, nothing remarkable, too thin if anything, the nose high-bridged, cheekbones too prominent perhaps, but it wasn't a face betraying ruthless pursuit of goals, was it? Or had that transition occurred without her noticing it? Her almost violet eyes were a bit startling, maybe, set as they were in such dark lashes, but certainly her hair didn't give the impression of ruthless determination; it sprang every which way, totally unsuppressed. Maybe nature didn't reflect her looks, or maybe because of her rather unruly appearance she had unconsciously made the inner person more. . .what? Efficient? And there you are, Hilary, back to that word again! And that's a fine self-deception, she mentally scolded; it has nothing to do with your looks, as you very well know. Only those thoughts were too uncomfortable to contemplate so she pushed them back into her mind. Picking up the iron, she kept her attention very firmly on her task as though ironing the collar of her blouse needed every bit of her concentration.

'Rankle, did it, Hilly?' he asked softly.

'No,' she denied stiffly. 'Why should it? I don't give a damn what people think of me, especially you,' she retorted almost inaudibly.

'Don't you even mind that the villagers think you unapproachable?'

'No.' It was what she wanted, wasn't it? To be left alone, and yet didn't they deserve better? They'd been unbelievably kind to her, not that it was any of his buiness—he wasn't one of the villagers, just a visitor. 'Anyway, I'm not unapproachable,' she defended, 'just contained.'

'Haughty,' he contradicted, 'as though you're looking down your nose at us lesser mortals.'

'I don't!' she denied vehemently. 'I don't look down on anybody!'

'I didn't say you did,' he explained patiently. 'I said you look as though you do.'

'And no longer part of the human race. Well, it's only been a. . .' she began, then hastily broke off, biting her lip.

'A year?' he asked softly.

Slamming down the iron, she glared at him. 'My God, you've only been here a week, and already. . .'

'I know all there is to know about you?' he finished for her. 'It's a small village, Hilary; people—talk.'

'Gossip, you mean!' she declared bitterly.

'All right, gossip, but it's not meant unkindly. They're concerned about you. Yes, they are,' he insisted when she snorted.

'Well, even if they are, that doesn't give you the right to poke your nose into my affairs!'

'True!' he agreed affably.

Oh, God, she thought wearily, how could you

cope with a man who kept agreeing with you? Who was being deliberately thick-skinned? 'Just go away, will you?' she entreated wearily. 'Please? I just want to be left in peace, I need time. . .'

'You've had time; how much more do you need, for goodness' sake? You can't go on wearing the willow forever.'

'I'm not wearing the willow! And will you please stop pretending you care about me? The only possible reason for your unwarranted interference is boredom! And what's so terrible about wanting to be left alone? To want to become a more complete person, one not likely to be hurt?'

'Nothing, but you're in danger of turning it into an art form. You can't spend the rest of your life running from one disastrous affair. Life goes on, Hilly.'

'I know it does! And I'm living it! Or trying to, but I'd have a great deal more chance of success if people didn't keep trying to drag the whole sordid mess out into the open. I want to forget it, not hold a post-mortem! And, if I'm so terrible, why on earth do you keep coming round?

'Because I'm a masochist?' he asked with a humorous smile. 'But while I'm on the subject——'

'Oh, God. Now what? Well, go on,' she prompted with soft sarcasm when he remained silent. 'What?'

'Your hair.' When Hilary cast her eyes up in supplication, he laughed. 'You should always leave it loose like that—it makes you look softer, more feminine. When you screw it up on top of your head it makes you look like that woman out of South Pacific, the one who sings "Bali Ha'i" or whatever.'

'Why don't I just wear a bag over my head?' she asked. 'Then no one will have to be put out by my looks.'

'Oh, that's a good idea,' he agreed earnestly, and Hilary gave a reluctant smile. 'That's better,' he approved. 'Now you look. . .' His eyes crinkling, he shook his head, refusing to complete the sentence. 'Actually, hard as it may be for you to believe, I did come for a reason.' Removing one hand from behind his back, he held out a small bowl. 'Sugar?' he asked hopefully.

With an expressive grimance, she nodded towards the far wall. 'It's in the cupboard—as you very well know.'

'Mm.' With a chagrined smilke that was patently false, he flipped open the top cupboard door nearest him, took out the packet of sugar and carefully filled his bowl before returning the packet to the shelf. Leaning his very broad shoulders against the door-frame, he promptly returned his gaze to Hilary.

'My nephew is coming,' he informed her blandly.

'How nice. Needs sweetening, does he?' she

asked with a defiant show of sarcasm. 'And I suppose you don't have any milk either.'

'Oh, yes, I have milk, Hilly.'

'Hilary,' she corrected between her teeth. 'My name is Hilary.'

'Hilary,' he agreed quietly, his voice full of laughter, 'but if you could manage a teensy bit of custard powder. . .?'

'My God,' she burst out in exasperation, 'don't you ever buy anything?'

'Well, yes,' he murmured, his brow furrowed as though he were taking her question seriously, 'I bought some——'

'Don't!' she yelled, quite unable to help herself. 'Don't you dare give me a damned shopping-list. The question was rhetorical!' Her lovely eyes reflecting her confusion and hurt, she wailed helplessly, 'I don't want you here.'

'I know,' he admitted softly and she stared at him in astonished disbelief.

'Then why? Why are you doing this to me?' Gazing into grey eyes that seemed incredibly gentle and soft, she forgot all about his reasons for being there, forgot everything except this infuriating giant who was slowly but surely destroying her peace of mind, 'Why?' she whispered.

'Because. . .' Glancing quickly down, he seemed to change his mind. Spreading his hands helplessly, he offered, 'Just because,' he concluded lamely.

'Because you pity me?' she asked, incensed.

'Pity you? Good God, no! From what I can gather, you're well rid of the bastard!'

She knew that, dammit! But being well rid of him and being able to forget him were horses of a very different colour! Averting her eyes, she stared down at the ironing-board, then, for the lack of any other brilliant alternatives, began to slowly move the iron back and forth across her blouse, her face shuttered.

'Come out and play, Hilly, before it's too late,' he encouraged softly.

'I don't want to come out and play,' she denied fretfully. 'I just want you to go away Mr—eh—well, whatever. . .'

'Leo,' he said on a choke of laughter.

Looking up in surprise, she found he had one eyebrow raised as though waiting for her to make some sarcastic comment, which success-fuly ensured that she didn't do any such thing. Besides, she couldn't think of one; all she could think was that he didn't look like a Leo. Leos were blond and, well, lionish, she supposed. But if she had to liken him to anything it would be an overgrown teddy bear in determined pur-suit of his honey. Only why was he being so determined in the face of her rudeness? That was what she wanted to know.

Without saying anything further, he shifted his enormous shoulders more comfortably against the door-frame as though settled for the rest of the day, and moved his eyes to her mouth almost as though he was waiting for her to speak again, she thought, feeling thoroughly disgruntled. Tightening her lips as though afraid they might widen against her will, she then found she couldn't bear the ensuing silence.

'If there's nothing else,' she prompted haughtily, 'I'm sure you have lots of things to do before your nephew arrives.'

'Nephew?' he queried blankly. 'Oh, nephew,' he agreed, and a gleam of laughter lit his eyes, which thoroughly unnerved her. With a slow smile that gave his face quite extraordinary charm, he picked up his bowl, waved a languid hand, then turned and ambled back across the garden, his borrowings clutched ridiculously to his large chest.

Releasing a shaky little sigh, she put the iron back on its stand with a hand that shook. Why couldn't she just ignore him? she wondered despairingly. Why did she have to rise to his taunts? Justify herself? She didn't want his constant intrusion into her life. Didn't want him to know about her.

Feeling restless and irritable and in no mood for doing her ironing, she pulled the plug out with an angry little jerk. Perhaps she'd go for a walk, see if any driftwood had collected in the bend of the river. She needed some more wood for her carving if she was to complete all the 'little comforters', as she called them, during her three-week holiday away from the travel agents where she worked, small, smooth-shaped pieces of wood, lovingly carved and polished by herself to fit easily into the palm and which, much to her surprise and delight, were eagerly accepted by the large rehabilitation hospital in the next town that cared for the blind and mentally sick. She'd always enjoyed using her hands and gained immense satisfaction from shaping and moulding whatever material came to hand, be it driftwood, clay or plasticine, and had come quite accidentally into using boxwood and rosewood which gave a smoother warmer feel than other woods or stone. From being a simple pleasure that had helped take her mind off her troubles, it had now gone a long way towards restoring her rather battered pride. Being useful, even if only in a small way, was a marvellous booster of confidence.

Dismissing the irritating Leo from her mind, she ran lightly upstairs to collect a thick sweater and to pull on heavy shoes before setting off across the boggy field behind the cottage towards the bend in the river. As she wandered slowly along, her eyes on the sluggish water, she suddenly spotted a heavy branch that looked to be oak. Grasping a handful of bulrushes to steady herself, she leaned precariously out to grab it. Just as her fingers touched it, one foot slid from under her and she lot her balance. With an involuntary yell of alarm she tumbled forward and sprawled full length in the muddy water.

With an exclamation of disgust, she pushed herself to her knees and flung the offending branch as far as she could in temper at her own stupidity. Crawling forward because that seemed marginally safer than trying to get to her feet, she focused startled eyes on a pair of muddy wellington boots. Flinging her head upwards, she stared at Leo, and several seconds must have elapsed before she had the gumption to grasp his extended hand. Hauling herself out, she muttered a disgruntled, 'Thank you—and if you dare laugh,' she threatened as she saw his lips twitch, 'so help me, I'll kill you!'

Giving one of his slow smiles which so infuriated her, he tugged her up on to the bank.

Standing awkwardly on one leg, she looked round for her other shoe and could only watch in helpless despair as she saw it slowly sink. Terrific. Feeling stupid and wretched and impossibly wet, her cord trousers clinging horribly to her legs, her sweater feeling ten times heavier with the weight of water, she glared ahead of her as Leo courteously helped her back on to firm ground. Of all the damned stupid, ridiculous things to have done! And why, why did it have to be him who found her? Her arms held out to her sides, she stared at her wet and muddy palms. God alone knew what she must look like—a creature from the black lagoon probably—and suddenly, unexpectedly, she began to chuckle. Turning her head, she stared straight into Leo's eyes. With her own brimful of mirth, the haze of tears making them shine like glowing amethysts in her dirty face, she was quite unaware of how extraordinarily lovely she looked. But gradually, as she registered his lack of response, she sobered, her eyes growing wary again. Feeling hurt and bewildered, she looked away, then squealed in alarm as he swung her up into strong arms.

'Put me down!'

'Don't be childish, Hilary,' he reproved mildly, 'you can't walk with only one shoe.'

'Of course I can!'

Halting, he stared down into her mutinous face, his grey eyes calm. 'Not only is the field littered with broken glass,' he explained patiently, 'but sharp flints, rocks and goodness knows what else. Do you want to cut your foot open?'

'Of course I don't! But——'

'But you don't like me touching you. I know.'

Hastily averting her face, she stared blindly down. So he *did* know she disliked his touch. Did he also know why? That the feel of his strong arms made her feel small and vulnerable? That his warm breath on her face churned up her insides to such an extent that she was forced to lie rigid? Becoming embarrassingly aware of the awful smell emanating from her sodden clothing, she closed her eyes in defeat. In her misery she didn't even notice where he was taking her until they were on his back doorstep.

When he halted and put her gently down, she mumbled hastily, 'Thank you. I can walk home quite easily from here.'

'Don't be silly,' he reproved, 'you'll catch your death.' Before she could stop him, he'd opened the back door and ushered her through. Kicking off his muddy wellingtons, he walked across to the towel rail on the far side of the old-fashioned kitchen. Bringing back a large towel, he spread it on the floor. 'No need to worry about making a mess,' he comforted her, his expression very, very bland. 'Take your shoe off and stand on the towel.'

'I was not. . .' she began irritably, only to find herself talking to thin air as he ducked down and removed her shoe for her. She was so startled that she just stood there like a dummy, and then, before she quite knew how it had happened, her wet sweater had been whipped over her head, a dry towel thrust into her hand and she was halfway into the hall.

'Shower's upstairs,' he told her solemnly. 'Put the rest of your clothes out on the landing; I'll rinse them through and put them in the drier. Don't be long, will you? I'll make the tea.' With another little push, he closed the kitchen door behind her.

Without causing a scene and making herself look even more ridiculous, she decided she had no choice but to do as she was told. Her lips set mutinously, she trudged up to the bathroom.

Stripping off the rest of her wet clothes, she bundled them out on the landing, then irritably turned on the shower and stepped beneath the hot jets. He'd done it again, she thought morosely, yet for a while, back there in the field, she'd felt almost like her old self, the person she had been before Ryan had come into her life. Would it have hurt Leo to have shared her laughter? Just smiled, maybe? And yet for a moment in the kitchen she thought she'd caught a fleeting expression almost of smugness on his face, as though something had pleased him. Yet why on earth should it?

Cross with herself for even trying to work out his peculiar behaviour, she climbed out and dried herself. Rubbing her hair hard to get rid of most of the wetness, she unhooked a navy towelling robe from behind the door and wrapped herself in its soft folds. It held the faint tang of a man's aftershave and she hugged it to her for a moment before realising how ridiculous she was being. It didn't smell like something the colonel would use, so she guessed it was Leo's, and for some silly reason that made her feel vulnerable, as though she'd lost her identity. Sighing, wishing she felt more confident, more able to cope, she madre her way slowly downstairs.

Reluctant to face Leo, she idled to admire Colonel Newman's family portraits. He hadn't said he was going away and renting his house, which was odd because they'd been chatting in the village not two days before he'd disappeared and Leo taken up residence. When she reached the bottom of the rather ornate staircase she hovered uncertainly for a moment, then with a

defiant toss of her head she marched into the
shabby splendour of the lounge before coming
to a lame halt. Leo was crouched before the fire,
and she had the odd fleeting impression of
power, a sort of unconscious arrogance that was
only magnified when he turned his head. It was
a face that was interesting rather than classically
handsome, she thought, staring blankly at him.
A determined jaw that was balanced by the
broad forehead, softened at the moment by the
unruly fall of hair. There was strength and an
inner confidence reflected in those steady grey
eyes that she suddenly realised were subjecting
her to a thorough appraisal. Tightening the belt
of the robe self-consciously, she looked quickly
away when he gave a small, amused smile.

'You look like a little blue bush-baby. . .'

'Bush-baby?' she echoed faintly, then gave a
rueful grimace. 'Thanks, although I suppose I
ought to be thankful it wasn't a kiwi you likened
me to.'

'They're from New Zealand.'

'I know where they're from, Leo! I don't need
a geography lesson.'

'Don't you?' he teased, his grin widening. 'All
right, but I was merely pointing out that I would
hardly liken you to an animal or bird from New
Zealand when I'm Australian.'

'Australian?' she repeated with a frown. 'But
Mr Green in the shop said you were from
Auckland.'

'Well, I'm sorry,' he apologised lightly, his

eyes glittering with amusement, 'but I'm defi-
nately an Aussie. Does it matter? Don't you like
New Zealanders? Is that the reason for the
antipathy towards me?'

'What?' she asked, her frown deepening. 'No,
of course not! Don't be ridiculous! I just didn't
know, that's all.' But it did matter—or did it?
Oh, God, why was it that whenever she was
around this man her wits went begging? But if
he was Australian——

'Come and sit by the fire and get warm,' he
instructed, interrupting her thoughts.

With a defeated sigh she went to perch on the
leather pouffe. 'I hope you didn't mind my
borrowing your robe,' she said awkwardly.

'Why would I mind?' he asked gently.

'I don't know,' she confessed with a small
inadequate sigh as she turned to look at him.
Expecting to find a look of mockery on his face,
she was disconcerted to see that it held nothing
of the sort. He looked. . .well, she didn't really
know how he looked. Sort of pleased, and kind.
Thoroughly confused, she turned her head and
stared blindly down at the fire.

'How much holiday do you have left?' he
asked quietly.

'Less than two weeks,' she mumbled without
looking at him, then wondered suspiciously
why he wanted to know. Turning her head, she
demanded, 'Why?'

'No particular reason, just idle curiosity. Oh,
Hilly, am I so very hard to talk to? Your clothes

won't be dry for a while yet; can't you at least meet me halfway?'

Flushing guiltily, she gave a quiet apology. 'I'm sorry, I think I've rather got out of the habit of talking to people.'

'Then now's a good chance to break yourself of it,' he encouraged gently. 'So, back to work in two weeks or so and then where?' he continued in the same quiet voice.

'What?' she asked blankly.

'The colonel said you worked for a travel agency as an assessor of foreign locations. I just wondered where you were off to next.'

'Oh.' Trust the colonel to give him chapter and verse. And they said women gossiped! 'I'm not quite sure, Rome, I think; the agency are thinking of starting up cultural tours—Rome, Athens, that sort of thing. I'm to check out hotels, tour facilities. The Italians like to run their own tours, rather like a closed shop, so I need to find an operator willing to take on more tourists. Apparently it gets pretty crowded in the Colosseum.' When he laughed, she turned to give a small smile.

'Well, as long as no one throws you to the lions.'

'No,' she agreed inadequately.

'And then on to Athens?' he persisted quietly.

'Maybe; not sure yet—it's still only tentative. It's only because I know Rome quite well that they've asked me—Athens I don't know at all.'

'It's well worth a visit,' he informed her, 'but

not in the height of summer—too hot,' he grinned.

'And that from an Aussie?' she was startled into answering, then went pink when he gave her a look of what she could only describe as approval.

'Mm, different sort of heat. I'll go and pour the tea. Do you take sugar?'

'Two, please.' Glancing at him, she was tempted to tease him about the sugar he had borrowed earlier, but if she did that it would amount to a tacit admission that he was right about her behaviour. It would widen the chink in her armour—and she didn't want it widened.

With a small smile that proved he knew very well what she had been thinking, he went out, and she tried to relax her tense muscles. Behave normally, she scolded herself. But it had been so long since she'd talked, really talked to anyone, that now she felt stiff and awkward. Once she would have chatted, laughed, teased him, asked where he came from, what he did; now she found it hard to summon up the energy to care. She just wanted to escape back to her cottage, her solitary existence.

When he returned, carrying two mugs, she took hers automatically then stared down into the swirling liquid.

'Your parents and brother are in Australia, aren't they?' he asked quietly as he perched on the arm of the safa, his mug held between large palms.

Feeling a shiver of apprehension, a cold finger touching her back, she glanced at him. Was this the crux of the matter? What he'd been leading up to all week? Yet his face held curiously little expression, certainly not one of avid curiosity, or knowledge.

'They moved out just over a year ago,' she admitted flatly. 'Went out for my brother Martin's wedding and decided to stay.' And if she hadn't met Ryan, Ryan with the lovely smile, Ryan the leech, she would have been out there with them. 'Why did you want to know?' she asked suspiciously.

'No reason,' he said easily as he sipped his tea, his eyes watching her steadily over the rim of the mug. 'Just curious; someone mentioned it, that's all.'

'Who?' she demanded. 'The colonel again?'

'I don't remember,' he denied blandly. 'Which part did they go to?'

'North-west, Port Headland way,' she said dismissively, then felt forced to ask, 'Why? Do you know it?'

'Heard of it,' he murmured with apparent indifference. 'More tea?'

'No, thank you,' she said shortly, and was then thwarted—deliberately, she was sure—in her intention to probe further by his bland, 'I'll see if your clothes are dry.'

Coincidence? she wondered blindly. Or was she being paranoid? Australia was a big place; no real reason to suppose he knew her parents, and yet why did she keep getting this feeling of being manipulated?

She didn't actually hear him come back into the room; it was just the feeling of being watched that alerted her to his presence, and she turned her head warily. For a big man, he always seemed to move so silently, like a cat hoping to catch a mouse. Her clothes were folded neatly over one arm and she got to her feet to take them.

'Your shoe is still very wet. . .'

'Well, it won't matter for the few yards back to the cottage. . .'

'But no need to be uncomfortable if you can avoid it,' he said smoothly. 'I'll get the car out.'

Still staring at him, she asked bluntly, 'Do you know my parents?'

'Know them?' he asked, his eyebrows arching in surprise. 'Why should I know them?'

'I don't know,' she sighed, as misery and hurt washed over her again.

'You miss them, don't you?' he asked gently, and she gave an unhappy little nod. 'Then why on earth don't you go out to visit them?'

'I will!' she said defensively. One day, when she had enough money. The truth was she couldn't even afford to go to London, let alone Australia.

'Do they know? About Ryan?' he persisted with blunt deliberation. 'That he loved you and left you, taking all your savings with him?'

Staring at him in shock, her eyes blank and

far too bright, she burst out, 'My God! The colonel *has* been busy, hasn't he? Does the whole village tell every complete stranger that arrives all about me? Point me out as an oddity?' Her eyes filling with tears, she shrugged away as he went to put a gentle hand on her shoulder. 'I want to get dressed and go home!'

After staring at her for a few seconds in silence, he finally nodded and went out, leaving her to dress.

CHAPTER TWO

WHEN Hilary walked out into the hall, she found Leo waiting by the front door. 'All right?' he asked quietly.

'Yes. Shall we go?'

After a searching glance at her, he led the way out and helped her into the Land Rover.

Sinking down into the seat, she stared blindly through the windscreen, her thoughts on her distant family. Leo made it sound so easy. Go out. But how could she? How could she confess that they'd been right about Ryan? That not only had he stolen her savings, but the money Aunt Jane had left her when she'd died? They'd have been worried sick about her, and what could they do so many miles away? If she'd confessed at the beginning it wouldn't have been so bad, but how could she tell them now? Almost a year later?

'All it takes is a phone call, Hilary,' Leo said quietly as he slipped in beside her, his hands resting on the wheel, his face turned towards her. 'Or a letter.'

'No,' she denied obdurately.

'Why? I don't understand why you should feel ashamed when you were the innocent victim. . .'

'I don't feel ashamed,' she denied irritably, 'and I don't want to talk about it. . .'

'Then you should. Is it the fact of the money? Or the fact that he fell out of love with you——?'

'He never fell out of love with me because he wasn't ever *in* love with me!' she burst out vehemently. 'If he had it might have been easier to bear. The reason he asked me out, dear Leo, was because he had overheard some of the girls from the agency talking about the money Aunt Jane left me—wasn't it wonderful? Wasn't I lucky?'

'Heard where?' he asked, puzzled.

'In the pub round the corner from the office. Do you know, I bet that's where half the burglaries or crimes are hatched? In pubs. People overhear conversations, what people have bought, what money they have. People are so indiscreet!' she bit out. 'All he had to do was follow them back to the agency, come in as though wanting to book a holiday, and there was gullible little Hilary all ready and waiting to fall in love. Hysterical, huh?'

'No, Hilary, it isn't in the least hysterical. Go on.'

'Go on where?' she asked bitterly as she stared blindly through the mud-spattered windscreen. 'How could I have let that bastard make love to me?' she demanded violently. 'How could I have been taken in by his charm?'

'Because he was clever. Do you think you're the only one to be conned by experts?'

'No, of course I don't. But—oh, Leo, he was so damned plausible! He asked me out, and I was more than pleased to accept. Tall, tanned, golden hair, and those blue eyes so full of honesty and humour that I thought him a warm, generous man. And so he was, on other people's money. He overruled my objections about getting engaged so soon after meeting; soothed my worries about parting from my family—we could save up, go and visit them. So we got engaged and waved my family off to Australia; he knew of a little cottage we could buy not far from his boat yard—his boat yard,' she said disparagingly with a little snort of disgust. 'He was a hired hand. And naturally he didn't have quite enough money to buy it. . . "Oh, use mine," I said blithely—which, of course, he did, and put the property in his own name so that when he sold it out from under me there would be no legal come-back! And then, *then*, I actually compounded my stupidity by furnishing it and moving in!' And Ryan had spent more than one night under the roof with her, she remembered in bitter anguish. God, she must have been the prize dummy of all time.

'And when you came back from taking a party of tourists round Paris, it was to find it had been demolished,' he concluded quietly.

'Yes.'

'How?' he asked quietly.

'How?' she exclaimed in astonishment. 'What do you mean, how?'

'Well, it isn't that easy to have property demolished——'

'It is when it's unsafe!' she burst out.

'And was it?' he persisted.

'How the hell should I know?' With an irritable little gesture of her hand, she leaned back and said more quietly, 'It didn't look unsafe, but he had it surveyed, and, whether the surveyor was in his pocket or no, a report was written to that effect. That's why we couldn't get a mortgage, or so he said. With hindsight, I begin to wonder. However, it cost little more than the price of the land—a real bargain,' she parodied in a bitter little voice. 'So if we rebuilt it in a more palatial style we could make a real killing when we sold it. Although how we were supposed to be able to afford to rebuild, I had no idea, but whenever I queried anything he would just laugh and tell me to leave it all to him.'

'Which, of course, you did, because you trusted him.'

'Yes.'

'So you weren't entirely surprised to find it gone?'

'No, I suppose not. Not at first. I was just annoyed that he'd chosen to do it while I'd been away. I assumed he'd found us somewhere else to live while it was being rebuilt. It didn't take me long to find out otherwise. There *was* no other accommodation; neither was there any trace of Ryan. I had no money apart from my wages, no clothes, belongings, nothing. A house-clearance firm had cleaned the place out before it was knocked down. The police were very kind, sympathetic, and, even if they didn't say so, it was quite clear what they thought. Gullible. Oh, they would make a show of looking—taking my belongings was, after all, theft—but would I really prosecute my. . .lover? If it hadn't been for the colonel letting me have this cottage for a peppercorn rent, God knows where I'd be.'

'How did the colonel come into it?'

'Oh, he was the big Pooh-Bah. When I came back and found the cottage demolished, naturally in distress and amazement, I asked around in the village. The whole sorry story came out, the colonel was sent for—and here I am,' she finished lamely.

'So you write to your family, keeping up a pretence that all is well with your world? And don't they wonder why you've never married him?'

'Of course they do! Or did,' she qualified— the last few letters hadn't mentioned him at all.

When Leo made some small movement, she was suddenly brought back to the present and became moritifyingly aware that she had just emptied her heart to a virtual stranger. Biting her lip, she said in a stifled voice. 'Can we go now?'

For answer, he fired the engine and drove her quickly and silently back to the cottage.

'Thanks,' Hilary muttered ungraciously. Grabbing her wet shoe, she fled. Running inside, she quickly closed the door and leaned back against it, tears flooding her eyes. 'Damn,' she whispered. 'Oh, damn it all to hell and back!'

With a loud sniff, she climbed wearily up to her bedroom. Sinking down on the edge of the bed, she sat, head in hands. Talking to Leo had brought it all back, the hurt, the desperation, the painful break with her family. And all because of Ryan. From the very first time she'd taken him down to meet her family, she had seen that they hadn't liked him. Oh, they'd been polite, made him welcome, but they hadn't trusted him. And Ryan hadn't liked them. For a while they had all pretended, but it had been like walking on broken glass. Mother had never mentioned him by name but had been overly gushing, always a sign that she didn't like someone. Mike, her stepfather, had been his usual amiable self, but even he had treated Ryan almost warily. And, if she wrote now telling them they'd split up, they'd expect her to go out to Australia, and how could she with no money? Not only were her savings gone, but so was Aunt Jane's legacy and the money Mike had pressed on her as an early wedding present. . . If she could have admitted her folly at the beginning it would have been all right, but the longer it went on the harder it became. She knew it must hurt her mother thinking that her only daughter was living with a man, a man, moreover, that she didn't like.

Pushing the hurt and the memories away, she got heavily to her feet and stripped off her uncomfortable clothes before dressing in soft jeans and a white sweat-shirt. She dragged her hair ruthlessly back and tied it with a narrow ribbon. Staring at her white face in the bedroom mirror, she conjured up an image of her family. Her mother; was she still slim? Or had she begun to put on weight? Had the soft dark hair gone grey? And Mike; was he still kind, gentle? And her brother Martin? Was he truly happy in his marriage to an Australian girl?

With a long, unhappy sigh, Hilary bundled up the clothes she had discarded and carried them downstairs. When she walked into the kitchen she came to a shocked halt. Leo was sitting at the kitchen table, his large frame almost dwarfing the little wooden chair, arms folded across his massive chest so that it pulled the material of his shirt impossibly tight.

Closing her eyes in defeat, she slumped back against the door-frame. 'Now what?'

Leaning back so that the chair creaked alarmingly, he held her watch up, dangling it to and fro by the strap, his expression neutral. She dumped her dirty clothes on the floor and walked across to take it, then grunted with annoyance as he moved it out of her reach.

'I'm not in the mood for games, Leo,' she said shortly. 'Either give it to me or don't.'

With a slow thoughtful smile he moved it back towards her and she snatched it from his hand. 'Thank you,' she muttered ungraciously.

'My pleasure. I thought you might need it, or miss it—if it's valuable,' he drawled slowly, 'or of sentimental value.'

Giving him a sharp look, she turned away. It did have sentimental value; her mother had given it to her for her twenty-first birthday. Not that he could know that, she assured herself. It had been a lucky guess, that was all. She turned away and placed her watch on the shelf above the sink, then, bending, began stuffing her clothes into the washing-machine. If he was so thick-skinned that he couldn't see when he wasn't wanted then that was his problem. If she tried to evict him an undignified struggle would only ensue and she wouldn't give him the satisfaction. Biting her lip hard to prevent herself screaming at him to stop sitting there like some damned great Buddha she busied herself finding soap powder for the machine, and in her agitation knocked the packet over, spilling powder all over the floor.

'Now look what you've made me do!' she exclaimed agitatedly, then gasped in surprise when Leo got lazily to his feet, grasped both her elbows and lifted her out of the way. Each touch of each finger seemed to burn through her sweat-shirt, and her insides gave the most awful lurch as he held her easily above the floor, his eyes fixed steadily on hers. His slow smile seemed almost predatory, and Hilary felt a very odd sensation slide down her spine and curl round to her stomach, making her shiver. But most alarming of all was the feel of the hard-muscled thigh pressing against hers, and, for some reason she couldn't explain, she found it hard to drag her eyes away from his. And the longer he held her the weaker she felt.

'Put me down,' she whispered through dry lips, and only after what seemed an enternity did he slowly lower her to one side.

'Do you have a dustpan and brush?' he asked mildly, then gave a funny little grin that she was unable to interpret. He looked perfectly amiable, so why did she get this feeling of apprehension, as though he was playing some sort of waiting game?

'Where's your nephew?' she blurted stupidly as she suddenly, inconsequentially, remembered his earlier words about his nephew. 'You said he was coming to tea.'

'So he is,' he murmured. 'It isn't yet teatime.'

'It isn't?' she asked, feeling hypnotised.

'No. They'll be here soon, I expect.'

'They?' she asked on a breath of sound.

'Mm. He's coming with his mother, my sister. She's married to an Englishman; they live in Norwich,' he explained quietly, and then his eyes lowered momentarily to her mouth, and that one glance was like a caress. Hilary could feel his warm breath on her face, almost feel the warmth of firm lips against hers. He was taunting her—she knew that—but why? He made her feel threatened and vulnerable, yet she was quite unable to dredge up her previous dislike. A horrible weakness seemed to have invaded her limbs and it took a supreme effort to drag her attention back to the conversation.

'I can do it,' she mumbled almost inaudibly. Making an awkward little gesture towards the cupboard under the sink, she stepped back hastily as he bent to collect the dustpan and brush.

'But it was my fault; you said so,' he murmured on a thread of laughter.

As she stared down at him while he cleared up the mess, she wondered why she felt so outmanoeuvred. It had been such a stupid little exchange, the words in themselves meaning nothing, yet here she was, trembling like a colt. Giving him a look almost of apprehension, she retreated to lean against the wall, furious with herself for her reaction. She watched the play of muscles in his powerful back and she reluctantly admitted that he really was a magnificent specimen. Only she wasn't likely to be caught twice that way, she thought with a cynical little smile. Now that he wasn't looming over her, she felt more composed, and it would be a very long time before she ever took a stranger on trust again. Men like Ryan, and probably Leo, could have their pick of women, which made it even

more unbelievable that she had been so stupid
as to believe Ryan. Men like that did not go out
with girls like herself. She was no raving beauty,
didn't have a model-like figure—all she'd had
was some money. Now she didn't even have
that—just a few bitter memories. So what did
Leo want? Or maybe, as she'd taunted earlier,
his actions were governed by boredom. Yet
there seemed such knowledge in those grey
eyes, so much awareness, and she shivered
again as she recalled the whipcord strength in
that seemingly indolent frame.

When Leo put the brush and pan into her
arms, she blinked up at him, startled out of her
thoughts. Her eyes looked almost deep purple
in the dim kitchen as she stared at him.

'Thank you,' she managed lamely. When he
touched a gentle knuckle to her cheek, she
started; her breath lodged somewhere in her
throat and she could only stand helplessly as he
untied the ribbon securing her hair. His movements were slow and deliberate as he threaded
his fingers through the tangled strands, his eyes
on his task, and Hilary forgot to breathe
altogether, almost terrified by his touch.

'I don't bite, Hilary,' he said softly as he
returned his eyes to hers, his expression impossible to read.

'No,' she husked, and then he was bending
his head, and his mouth was touching hers, and
a funny little moan escaped her.

Lifting his head, Leo stared at her for long

moments, then, with another of his funny smiles, he murmured softly, 'Take care,' and he was gone.

Thoroughly shaken, she stared after him, the dustpan and brush cradled ridiculously in her arms, her mind completely blank, empty of thought or feeling. Giving a long shudder, she turned too quickly and white powder cascaded back to the floor. 'Oh, hell.' She bent and quickly swept the powder up again, then went outside to empty it into the dustbin. Had Leo really kissed her? Well, not a *kiss* precisely, she qualified; more a sort of caress. And why? Why, for goodness' sake? She'd been abominably rude to him since they'd first met. Abused his hospitality. . . It was crazy. And it was even more crazy to stand here daydreaming about it, she castigated herself. She'd been longing for peace and quiet so that she could get on with her carving, and, now that she had it, was standing here like a loon!

She made herself a sandwich and a cup of tea and carried them along to her workroom. Unlocking the door, she put her meal on the bench and donned the old smock she wore for working, then settled to sanding and smoothing the shapes she had already carved. Yet, even doing something she so loved, she couldn't quite banish the memories. Ryan, his charm, his humour; those impossibly blue eyes, the golden hair, the laughing handsome face; and the awful thing was that, if he came back tomorrow, she

didn't think she'd be immune, despite all that
he had done. She wanted to hate him, and on
one level she did, but part of her still wanted
him, and that seemed the worst betrayal of all.
Wanting a man who was such a louse.

Oh, Mum, she thought in despair, why did
you have to move? The letters they exchanged
were formal, just words on a piece of paper; the
warmth they had all shared for so long was
missing. It wasn't only due to the harsh words
they had exchanged over Ryan; she found it
hard to write naturally because of the lie she
was enacting. And Mike; always so good to her,
teasing her, making her feel special, as though
he had tried to make up for her real father's
dying when she was a baby; not wanting her to
feel left out when Martin had been born. And
she hadn't. So why couldn't she tell them? They
would understand, she knew they would, yet
she still couldn't squash her silly pride. Not only
had Ryan ruined her love and her trust, but he
had also made her a coward.

Yet slowly, as she worked, became more and
more absorbed in what she was doing, the
memories faded. Thoughts of Ryan and her
family retreated. She was unaware of the time
passing; there was only the comforting tick of
the grandmother clock in the corner to break the
silence. It had been a present from the colonel—
to keep her company, he'd insisted with his
gentle smile.

The smell of wood dye and shavings, more

pleasing to her than any perfume, filled the air as she worked contentedly on. The afternoon sun, peeping almost shyly though the small lattice window, touched her hair with gold and gave a warm glow to the range of tools lying on the littered bench. The little room seemed to conjure up a scene from the past, an almost timeless memory. The tools might be different, the craft diverse, but the feeling of serenity the room gave pleased and warmed her. For the first time in days Hilary felt at peace, the hurt and pain pushed aside for a while.

The small, soft sound took a while to register, and when it did she looked up, startled. Her violet eyes enormous, she stared at Leo in astonishment.

'I'm sorry,' he apologised softly, hastily, 'I know I'm intruding. I did knock and then became captivated. I'm sorry,' he repeated, and the smile he gave her was so gentle that the angry words she had been going to utter died, locked somewhere in her throat. 'I rescued your other shoe,' he added as he brought it out from behind his back.

When she didn't answer, only continued to stare at him helplessly, he continued hopefully, 'If I promise to remain mouse-like, may I stay and watch?'

'Mouse-like?' she asked huskily as she eyed his enormous frame. His bulk created an intimacy in the small workroom that made her wary, and the atmosphere, just for a moment, became charged, until he gave a little grimace which dispelled it.

'Elephant-like?' he queried with a grin. 'But, if I promise to be very quiet, may I stay?'

Not knowing how to refuse without sounding churlish, she looked down and absently began to smooth off the roughness of the article she was holding with an emery cloth. She was aware of him settling himself on the floor in the corner by the bench, then stiffened when he picked up one of her finished pieces. Watching from the corner of her eye as he curled his fingers round it, she was both pleased and astonished by the look of surprise that crossed his face.

When he lifted sleepy eyes towards her his voice, though still soft, was slightly incredulous. 'It's almost alive!' he exclaimed.

'Yes. Close your eyes,' she instructed quietly and, when he had obeyed, added, 'Feel it, move it in your hand, let your fingers read it.'

As he unhesitatingly obeyed, she watched him, really examined him for the first time in their acquaintance. Tried to see past the antipathy he always aroused in her. With his eyes closed, concentration firming his features, he didn't look in the least threatening. He had a strong face, the jaw almost rugged, the nose classically bridged. He had a nice mouth too, generous, well shaped, not thin-lipped like Ryan's, the thought intruded. Yet it was true, she thought, surprised; Ryan's mouth had been

thin. His smile too, now that she came to consider it, had been used for effect, to charm,
disarm. Frowning slightly, her face thoughtful,
she moved her eyes to Leo's large, capable
hands as they revolved the egg-shaped carving.

'What are you thinking?' she asked quietly.

When he looked up, his eyes curiously blank,
she mentally appreciated the picture he made.
The large body, relaxed and at ease, didn't look
at all incongruous crouched in the corner.
'Holland,' he said decisively. 'Yes, Holland.
With the sun slanting through the window,
giving your hair a reddish glow and shadowing
your face, you could be a Reubens come to life,
or maybe a Van Dyck. The dim, warm room, the
smell of turpentine and sawdust, has a Dutch
feel. . .'

'I meant,' she explained with a smile, 'the
thoughts generated by feeling the carving.'

'Yes, I know,' he agreed with a smile of his
own. Wriggling into a more comfortable
position, he held the carving up in front of him.
'Peace,' he said softly, 'warmth, contentment.
Extraordinary. You could make a fortune selling
them to stressed businessmen. How long have
you been doing them?'

'Not long; only since I've been here. Funny
how things turn out, isn't it? I met Dr
Johannsen, the senior therapist at the local hospital, when I was hunting for wood on the beach
at Cator. We got chatting, he seemed intrigued
by my descriptions of the carvings, and before I

quite knew where I was he'd accompanied me back here, appropriated a few of them, and disappeared. A few days later he came back, said they gave tactile pleasure to his patients, a little on the lines of worry beads, and off he went with a boxful.'

'And you've been supplying them ever since?'

'Yes.'

'So Ryan did have some uses.'

'What? Oh, Leo, don't!' she exclaimed unhappily. 'How many times do I have to tell you that I don't want to talk about him?'

'As many times as it takes for you to realise that shutting him out will only keep him in,' he insisted firmly. 'If you keep trying to pretend he didn't exist, you're letting him win. Your withdrawal, your unhappiness is a victory for him.'

'Which is still none of your damned business!' Getting agitatedly to her feet, she strode across to him and practically snatched the carving out of his hand.

'Tsk, tsk,' he taunted as he stood up, 'and losing your temper with me won't solve your problems. Come out of your ivory tower, Hilary, before it's too late, before you really turn into the arrogant bitch that at the moment you're only emulating.' With a mocking smile for her look of speechless outrage, he wandered out.

Slamming her tools down on the bench with almost enough force to break them, she flung the carving back into its box, then aimed a kick at it. How dared he called her an arrogant bitch?

How dared he? And it wasn't true—she wasn't
in the least arrogant! And what the hell had
happened to the mild, gentle humour he'd been
displaying since he'd arrived? Well, it hadn't
taken him long to show his true colours!

In sudden determination to have the last
word, she chased after him. Flinging open the
front door, she yelled to his retreating back, 'I
am not arrogant! And, even if I am, it has
nothing whatever to do with you!'

Receiving no answer, Hilary went back inside
and slammed the door. Interfering bastard. In
no mood now to finish her work, she stalked
along to the kitchen. It wasn't fair. Why couldn't
people just leave her alone? Feeling a wave of
dizziness, she slumped defeatedly at the kitchen
table. It was probably hunger, and she supposed
she ought to eat something, only she didn't feel
very hungry. In fact, she never felt very hungry.
She'd lost an awful lot of weight this last year,
and these recurring dizzy spells were probably
her body's telling her to buck up, but they were
slightly worrying all the same. If it had happened to anyone else she'd have told them to
snap out of it, to stop feeling sorry for themselves. So easy to give advice to other people,
she thought as her mouth twisted with self-
mockery. Perhaps she should go back to
London; the travel agent would no doubt trans-
fer her back again if she asked. Probably be glad
to get rid of her, she thought gloomily, then

looked up sharply as someone rapped at the back door.

Oh, now what? Getting tiredly to her feet, she yanked open the door and then just stood there, staring helplessly.

'Hi,' Leo said sheepishly.

Briefly closing her eyes, she sagged defeatedly against the door-frame. 'What do you want?'

When he held up a bottle and two glasses, she felt a strong desire to go into hysterics. He must have practically sprinted to his house, grabbed the bottle and glasses and sprinted back again. Why? 'Why?' she demanded.

'I thought it might improve your disposition,' he said outrageously. 'I've tried being polite. . .'

'Polite?' she exclaimed in disbelief. 'You're never polite! And my disposition or lack of it has nothing whatever to do with you! If you don't like it, stay away!'

'Can't do that,' he drawled languidly. Pushing past her, he walked through to the lounge.

'Why can't you?' she asked, incensed, as she slammed the door and hurried after him.

'Because the colonel asked me to keep an eye on you.'

'He did what?'

'Asked me to keep an eye on you,' he repeated mildly as he skilfully opened the bottle of wine. He poured it into the glasses and handed her one with a mocking little bow that nearly made Hilary throw the liquid all over him. 'Cheers.'

Did he really think his behaviour to date could be called 'keeping an eye on her'? she thought in astonishment. Staring at him, she exclaimed helplessly, 'Leo, I don't want you here! I don't want this constant interference in my life. I just want to be left alone!'

'Why? Because some bastard cheated you? Took your virginity? Don't be so damned poor-spirited. Look at you. Go on, look!' he insisted. Putting down his glass and removing hers, he gripped her shoulders and propelled her to stand in front of the mirror. 'Go on, take a long, hard look. You're rude, arrogant——'

'No!' she broke in desperately as she tried to wriggle away.

'Yes! You never smile, you slap down all attempts at help or friendliness. You avoid the villagers, who've done their damnedest to help you! You've——'

Finally managing to wrench herself free, she turned and hit him. All the anger, frustration and hurt finally exploded into action in violent contrast to the lethargy that had been her constant companion for the past few months. Glaring at him, her eyes washed with impotent tears, she tried to push past him, only to be caught in a punishing grip.

'Don't touch me!' she yelled.

'Why? Because it reminds you of all you've lost? You're a damned little coward, Hilary, and I don't know why I bother with you! Look at this place! Look at it—dingy and dull like your-self.' Pushing her back into her chair, he gave her back her glass and it was a measure of her distress that she actually reached out and took it.

'Why are you doing this?' she whispered, her voice shaking.

'Because I hate waste,' Leo said simply.

He seemed quite unperturbed by her behav-iour, by being walloped across the face, and she watched in amazement as he calmly took his own glass and sat in the chair opposite. 'How much longer are you going to go on like this?'

'I don't know.' Gazing listlessly at the bubbles floating to the top of her glass, she took an experimental sip. Those bubbles were no more free than she was—yet didn't she at least have a choice? Raising her eyes, she stared at Leo. He too was staring down into his glass, his thoughts no happier than her own, judging by his brood-ing expression. The red mark on his cheek was fading and she was suddenly horrified by her uncontrolled outburst. 'I'm sorry,' she said bleakly.

'Well, at least it was positive,' he said ruefully as he put up a blunt-fingered hand to touch his cheek. 'That's what I like about you, Hilary; don't waste words, do you? Just lash out. Pity you didn't do that to Ryan.'

'Yes,' she agreed, then looked up, startled, as his words registered. 'Like?' she asked with a frown.

'Drink your wine,' he persuaded softly.

Sipping at the wine and finding it quite pleasant, she asked quietly, 'How long have you known the colonel? He didn't say anything to me about renting out his house. Not that there's any reason why he should,' she added hastily, 'But it seems a bit odd, all the same.'

'Mm. It was sudden,' he murmured blandly, but she noticed that he didn't comment on how long he'd known him. Before she could pursue it, he added, 'Come on, drink up, else I'll think you haven't forgiven me.'

'Much as you'd care,' she derided. 'How long are you over here for?'

'A few weeks. I came to visit my sister Gwen; she lives not far from herre.'

'Yes, so you said.' Then, finding she was curious, she asked, 'What do you do?'

'Do?' he echoed softly. 'He looked down and a faint smile touched his mouth. 'I'm in property. Buying, selling, that sort of thing. Do you still love him?' he asked, all in the same breath.

'Oh, for goodness' sake! Do we have to keep talking about him?' she demanded irritably.

'Yes. Do you?'

'I don't know,' she muttered. No one had ever asked her that. It had never seemed to occur to anyone else that she might still do so, and part of her self-loathing was due to the fact that she didn't know. Couldn't be sure that if he walked back in now she wouldn't still feel that leap of the heart, that curl of excitement. Feelings didn't stop because you told them to; you couldn't just turn them off. 'I don't know,' she repeated as she stared blindly down into her glass. 'I shouldn't. I should hate him, only it seems so unreal sometimes, as though none of it ever happened. I know it did, but sometimes I can't grasp the reality.'

'There's no shame in loving,' he pointed out with what sounded like total indifference. 'Did he love you well?'

'What?' she whispered, not entirely sure she'd heard him right.

'Was he a good lover? Thoughtful? Gentle?' he elaborated.

'I don't know! I'd never had a lover before, I have no comparison,' she said shortly.

'Nor since?' he asked gently.

'No!' Suddenly recalling an incident that had happened a few months previously, she gave a small, twisted smile. 'I almost did. A man who was on one of the tours asked me out. Funny, I don't even remember his name. I don't think I even liked him very much.'

'But he was a sop to your pride? Is that it? Proof that you were still attractive to other men?'

It wasn't something she'd consciously considered before, just buried the memory along with all the others, but, thinking about it now, she knew he was right. Her face sombre, she nodded. 'Yes, I think perhaps it was. To prove I wasn't totally lacking in appeal, I suppose. We went out for a meal, and when he took me home he wanted to come in. I stood there on my doorstep with him, and I actually considered it. I quite coldly and dispassionately thought about it. No feelings, no nothing. . .'

'But when it came right down to it, you couldn't do it,' he finished for her.

'No. It seemed sordid, and stupid.'

'Silly girl,' he commented.

Unsure whether he meant silly because she shouldn't have needed the confirmation, or silly because she wasn't likely to get it, she frowned. 'Why?' she demanded, finally deciding that she'd just been insulted. 'It was a normal reaction, wasn't it? I'd been hurt—the man I thought loved me had not only jilted me and stolen my money, but admitted that he hadn't wanted me in the first place. How the hell did you expect me to feel? Philosophical?'

Getting to her feet, angry and hurt all over again, she moved jerkily about the small room and only halted when Leo came up behind her and placed his palms on her shoulders to still her. Turning her, he stared down into her eyes that shone with a hint of tears.

'Don't cry for him, Hilly. He's not worth it.'

'They're not for him,' she denied stiffly, 'they're for me.'

'Why? Because you feel unloved? Unwanted?'

'Shouldn't I?' she asked huskily. 'Or isn't self-pity allowed either?' Staring blindly at the strong column of his throat, she sniffed. She had an almost overwhelming longing to be held against that hard chest, enfolded in strong arms, and that was more worrying than anything else. She didn't even like him, for heaven's sake. He was intrusive, irritating. . . With a shaky sigh, she moved her eyes up to his impassive face. 'Why are you doing this to me?'

'I want Hilary back,' he said simply.

'Back?' she echoed stupidly. 'How back? You didn't know me.'

'I catch a glimpse of her sometimes,' he said softly, his eyes gentle, warm. 'A fleeting look, a flash of laughter quickly gone. A gleam of humour, a moment of beautiful pommy arrogance.' With a slow smile for her look of astonishment, he added, 'The first time I saw you, I wanted to make love to you.'

'What?' she exclaimed shakily. 'Don't be so ridiculous!'

'Why is it ridiculous?' he asked mildly, one eyebrow raised.

'Because it is!' she insisted dismissively. 'You don't just see someone and think, Oh, boy, I'd like to go to bed with her. . .' Suddenly recalling some of her brother's youthful enthusiasms, she came to a lame halt. He'd once used almost those exact words, and she seemed to recall that she'd told him not to be so crude.

'I didn't say I wanted to go to bed with you, but that I wanted to make love to you; a subtle difference,' he chided, 'and I don't know why you should look so disbelieving—you have a lovely supple body. . . A man can imagine silken limbs twined with his, can't he? Imagine warm, loving arms? A full mouth moving under his——?'

'Stop it!' she commanded, her cheeks hot with embarrassment.

'Why? Don't you want to be desired?'

'There's a great deal of difference between being desired and having it spelled out!' she insisted awkwardly.

With a slow, teasing smile, he asked outrageously, 'So was he an eager lover, my little friend? Ardent and demanding?'

'It's none of your damned business!' she snapped half-heartedly, yet his words struck a raw nerve and she almost winced in pain, because Ryan had only been ardent at first; after that, it had been she who had made the advances. 'And I am not your little friend,' she muttered, feeling terribly near to tears again.

Unexpectedly, Leo drew her into his arms and rested his head on hers. He felt warm and solid, safe, and, so long as she couldn't see the mockery that sometimes filled his eyes, she could pretend, couldn't she? That he was a friend as he had intimated? She heard him whisper something against her hair which she thought sounded like 'bastard' but she must have misheard, because why would he say that? Ryan's behaviour was nothing to do with him. As she let her breath out on a long sigh Hilary moved reluctantly away. Avoiding his eyes, she said quietly, 'It's late.'

'Yes, time you were in bed. Finish your wine,' he said easily as he handed back her glass, 'and then go get some sleep.' Touching a gentle finger to her nose, he moved to the door. 'Night, Hilary.'

'Night,' she echoed. And that was it? Mission accomplished? The colonel's instructions carried out? Feeling unutterably depressed, she wandered round the empty cottage that seemed to echo with loneliness. Funny how she'd never noticed it before. Sipping her wine, she stared round her. She'd never noticed how shabby everything was either until Leo had pointed it out. When she'd first moved in she hadn't cared about anything, certainly not her surroundings—they had been the least of her problems—and if the villagers hadn't so kindly donated her furnishings she'd probably still be existing in empty rooms. The two armchairs and the kitchen table were courtesy of the colonel. Cups, plates, saucepans and a little chest of drawers had been collected, or scounged, by Frank Green in the village shop. The only things she'd bought herself were the bed and bed-linen. Gradually, as she could afford it, she'd replaced her clothes, but nothing else. Leo was right; she had become a hermit. She'd blanked herself off, not caring about anything, barely participating in the life around her. She'd barely thanked the villagers, the shopkeeper, for their kindness and support. Had barely spoken to them, preferring to do her shopping in Norwich rather than run the gauntlet of village gossips in the local store. How much time do you need? he'd asked. How much indeed? Sighing, she finished her wine, then took both glasses out to the kitchen.

As she walked slowly upstairs, feeling incredibly tired, Hilary stared round her with new eyes. Depressing—that's what it was. Dark and gloomy. Like herself. Don't let him win, Leo had said, and he was right; that was precisely what she was doing. Wallowing in self-pity instead of fighting back. And why on earth had she allowed Leo to needle her into confiding in him? Didn't she have any pride? He was a virtual stranger, and in a few weeks would be going back to Australia. Undressing in the dark, she wondered why the thought depressed her. He probably told all women that he wanted them. It was probably the only way he could get one, she thought waspishly; the law of averages no doubt decreed that one at least would believe him, and how on earth could he want her when he'd said all those terrible things to her? Yet he'd been incredibly gentle after she'd hit him, and it was Leo's face in her mind as she fell asleep, not Ryan's.

She saw his sister and nephew next morning as she was loading her car with her carvings to take to the hospital. At least she assumed that was who they were as they walked with Leo down the lane towards her; she didn't wait to be introduced. Climbing quickly behind the

wheel, she gave a hasty wave before driving off.
Cowardly of her, no doubt, but for some odd,
undefined reason she didn't want to meet his
relatives. He was far too intrusive on his own,
without bringing his sister and nephew into it.
Only, if she thought she was going to escape
scotfree, she was mistaken; Leo was sitting on
her doorstep waiting for her when she arrived
back.

Turning off the engine, she stared at him in
exasperation. He looked utterly ridiculous,
lounging untidily back against the door. His face
was tilted to the weak sun, eyes closed. He was
wearing a disreputable pair of jeans that looked
as though they'd never seen an iron, and a grey
shirt, the sleeves rolled back as if it were
summer. He didn't even seem to be aware that
a chill north wind was blowing. Everyone else
was bundled up in thick sweaters, including
Hilary, and all the confused feelings she'd tried
to suppress the night before came tumbling back.

Swinging long jeans-clad legs out, she got to
her feet and slammed the car door. When he
didn't move or give any indication that he knew
she was there at all—although he must have
heard the car draw up and, unless he was deaf,
the car door slam—she marched across to him.
Standing in front of him, she glared disagreeably
down at the tousled brown hair.

'Avoiding me, Hilly?' he asked quietly without
so much as a twitch. When she remained silent,
he opened one eye to observe her mutinous face.

'If I thought I would have any chance of success, I probably would,' she said sarcastically. 'And you're blocking my door!'

'Ah, regretting your confidences of last night,' he stated. Opening the other eye, he regarded her stiff figure with amusement. He climbed lazily to his feet and stood to one side so that she could open the door, then followed her inside. Leaning in the kitchen doorway, he watched as she put the kettle on, then asked softly, 'When did Ryan tell you he only went out with you for the money?'

'What?'

'Last night you said——'

'Last night I said altogether too much!'

'And now you're regretting it,' he agreed, infuriatingly reasonable in the face of her temper.

'Oh will you go away?' she wailed irritably. 'You're driving me insane!'

'Good,' he retorted. Turning on his heel, he went out.

'Leo!' she yelled in exasperation, dashed after him and skidded to a halt as he stopped abruptly and turned. 'I think you must be the most irritating man I've ever had the misfortune to meet! What do you mean, "Good"?'

'Just what I said. Good. So, when did he tell you?'

'What difference does it make?'

'None, but it's been bothering me. You said you came back from France to find the cottage demolished and Ryan gone. So when did he admit that he only wanted your money?'

'Are you sure you're in property?' she demanded suspiciously. 'You sound uncommonly like a policeman to me, searching for evidence. Oh, all right,' she agreed wearily. If she didn't tell him he'd probably stand there all day. 'I got a letter from him a few days later, sent to the travel agents. Satisfied?'

'Where was it posted?'

'I don't know, do I? I didn't look. I just screwed it up and threw it away!'

'And it said what? That he'd never wanted you? That it was only ever your money?'

'Yes!' she hissed. 'And to tell my friends to be more careful where they discussed other people's affairs! Like in the local pub! Now will you go away?'

Nodding thoughtfully, he turned and left.

She let her breath out and went back to the kitchen to make the tea. Why on earth did he need to know all the damned details? What possible difference could they make now? Feeling irritable and out of sorts, she took her tea into the workroom, hoping her carvings might be as therapeutic to her as to the people she carved them for. It was hard to remember what her life had been like before Leo came, but, whatever it had been, it had to have been more peaceful than this. His constant invasion of her privacy was driving her to distraction. Why was he so damned nosy?

CHAPTER THREE

For once the work didn't soothe Hilary. Her mind kept wandering into speculation about Leo. Why did he keep probing about Ryan? He didn't really strike her as a particularly nosy person, just wanting to know things for the hell of it. So why? It nagged at her like an aching tooth. Or perhaps all Australians *were* like that, took an uncommon interest in everyone's affairs. Or he was bored. Life in a little Norfolk village was hardly riveting, so perhaps that was it, only it wasn't an explanation that satisfied her. There was also an odd, tingling excitement about their encounters, she admitted honestly. It wasn't that she looked forward to them exactly, but the fury he'd used to generate was gone.

Deciding it was pointless trying to work when her mind wouldn't settle, she put her things away. She'd have something to eat, go for a walk maybe—or paint the living-room, she suddenly decided. Getting quickly to her feet, she walked along the tiny hall to the back room. As she leaned in the doorway she surveyed the gloomy décor. The walls and ceiling were a sort of depressing brown. Years of grime from the coal fire had so discoloured the original paintwork

58

that it was difficult now to guess what colour it had been. Cream probably. The little village shop sold emulsion, she remembered, and maybe she could go into Norwich and buy new curtains, a bright chintzy print. Pursing her lips thoughtfully, she half closed her eyes as she tried to visualise how it might look. Certainly no worse than it did at present.

Once the decision was made, she was eager to begin. For the first time in a long while, she felt vital, enthusiastic. Her movements brisk and purposeful, she made herself some lunch, and actually forced herself to eat it. She quickly rinsed her cup and plate, collected her purse and jacket and almost ran out of the front door. As she turned into the lane leading to the village, she gradually slowed and came to a halt as she saw Leo descend from the local bus. For once he really looked quite smart, in well-cut grey trousers that emphasised the length of his legs and strength of his thighs, and a cream shirt that actually looked as though it had been ironed. Reluctant to face him, she hung back, waiting for him to move off.

Watching as he grinned up at the bus driver, said something and laughed, she felt a hollow ache inside. It had been a long time since she'd laughed, joined in a joke, been silly just for the hell of it. Leo was probably fun to be with, a great companion, a good friend, she thought, then gave a wry chagrined smile as he turned towards her as though he'd been aware of her presence all along—and she might have known he wouldn't do anything so obliging as to walk off. With that deceptively loose-limbed walk, he ambled towards her, and Hilary tried to picture him as a property developer and failed. He looked as though he might be a racing driver, or a round-the-world yachtsman, something exciting and challenging; certainly nothing so mundane as an estate agent.

'Hello,' she greeted fatalistically.

His eyes crinkling, he merely stood and watched her.

'What were you doing on the bus? Slumming it?'

'The Land Rover broke down on my way back from Norwich,' he explained with an air of bewilderment that was so patently false that Hilary gave another reluctant smile.

'That doesn't surprise me in the least,' she said drily. 'It looked as though it was on its last legs when you gave me a lift yesterday.'

'Hm. So, I wondered. . .'

'No,' she refused, knowing exactly what was coming next. 'Absolutely and categorically not! Apart from which I would think it highly unlikely that you would even get into my little car.' Eyeing his enormous frame with amused speculation, she suddenly grinned, not even aware that slowly, little by little, she was reverting to the old Hilary. 'Don't you?'

Giving her a long, slow appraisal that made

her wriggle uncomfortably, he asked softly, 'Decided to rejoin the human race?'

As she stared at him her face sobered. Feeling stupidly embarrassed, as though she'd been caught doing something she shouldn't, she looked jerkily away. 'I was going to the shop,' she explained awkwardly, 'to buy paint.'

'Paint?' he queried, as though it was an item he'd never come across, much as he might have sounded if she'd said she was going to buy a giraffe, she thought on a spurt of amusement.

'Yes, paint. I'm going to take your advice and brighten up the living-room.'

'Ah. Red?' he asked, a fascinating little smile tugging at his mouth.

'No, silly! White, or cream.'

'Of course, very cautious. Quite right, too; one step at a time.'

'Yes, well, I'd better go,' she murmured in confusion.

'Yes, and I must go to the garage.' Putting a companionable arm round her shoulders that made her shiver with awareness, he urged her in the direction of the village. 'I'll walk with you.'

'I could call into the garage for you,' she offered hastily, not too sure of the wisdom in allowing him to walk anywhere with her. Walking with him smacked of an intimacy she wanted to avoid, apart from which the sight of them together would prompt all sorts of speculation among the villagers.

'Stop trying to think of an excuse not to walk with me,' he whispered softly. 'I promise to behave.'

'That will make a change.'

Resigning herself to the inevitable, she walked quietly alongside him as he kept up a running commentary on all they passed or saw. The warmth of him against her side was making her feel more and more unsettled, and her answers to his comments were more than a little distracted. She wanted to shrug away from him but not prompt a discussion about her behaviour, which she no doubt would if she did.

There's Mrs Beeson,' he breathed softly. 'Want to give her something to talk about?'

'No, I do not!' she exclaimed, horrified. Mrs Beeson was the worst gossip in the village. What she didn't know, she made up. 'Leo,' she warned as he hugged her even more closely against his side, 'let me go!' Feeling a complete fool, she gave Mrs Beeson a lame smile as she tried to struggle free.

'You should be pleased,' he commented outrageously.

'Why?' she demanded.

'Because now she can talk about that nice Australian gentleman who's helping poor Miss Dawson to recover from her tragedy.'

The way he said it, almost putting it in inverted commas, made her give a reluctant smile. It was so exactly what Mrs Beeson would say. Anything of a supposedly unmentionable nature she gave added emphasis to by leaving a little pause, peering suspiciously around her as though someone might be listening, then saying the word, or sentence, in a theatrical stage-whisper. Trouble and tragedy were two of her especially favourite words.

When they reached the garage Leo left her to go and sort out the problem of the Land Rover, and Hilary continued on alone. Halting outside the little store, she took a deep breath to give herself courage before pushing open the door, then grimaced as the bell gave an important little ping which alerted everyone inside to her presence. Refusing to cower behind the racks as she usually did, she walked boldly along the centre aisle. She smiled at the few women clustered at the counter and acknowledged their somewhat surprised greetings, and was enormously grateful to Frank Green, the owner, for treating her as if she were a regular and valued customer instead of a virtual stranger.

His plump face breaking into a warm smile, he called, 'Be with you in a moment, Miss Dawson.'

'That's all right, I'll just wander round. I need some paint,' she explained awkwardly, which got the same astonished reaction she'd had from Leo. Didn't anyone ever buy paint, for goodness' sake? Avoiding their curious glances, she walked round to the hardware section and tried to shut her ears to the whispered conversations that suddenly broke out as soon as she was out

of sight. Well, she'd known it wasn't going to
be easy.

Peering round the end shelf as she heard the
doorbell ping again, she pulled a face as she saw
it was Mrs Beeson. Oh, hell, she had no doubt
hotfooted it to the store after seeing her with
Leo. Smiling to herself, she listened to the
hissed shushing that ensued as Mrs B. tried to
impart her news. Taking pity on them because,
despite her irritation with their constant pre-
occupation with her affairs, she knew it wasn't
meant maliciously, and they'd been enormously
kind after Ryan's defection, she walked back to
the counter.

'I think I need some advice, after all,' Hilary
said quietly as she walked up to the little group.
Injecting a note of surprise into her voice as
though she were only now aware of her presence, she greeted, 'Hello again, Mrs Beeson. I'm
going to paint the living-room. Only shall I use
eggshell? Vinyl? Or matt?' she queried. Beginning to feel like one of the characters from the
children's programme *Camberwick Green*, she
hastily suppressed the little involuntary twitch
of her lips. She wondered if she sounded as daft
as she felt, glanced slyly at Frank Green, and
they both burst out laughing.

'Well, now, that's a pleasure to see,' he
approved gruffly. He rummaged under the
counter and produced a colour chart, and, shov-
ing the display-case of cakes to one side he
flattened it out so that everyone could see and

comment as they saw fit. Obviously a serious decision like painting walls needed the input of as many people as possible. As they all bent over the chart, the shop door pinged again, and, as one, they all swung round to look, and Hilary froze in disbelief. From the cheerful babble of a moment ago, there was now total silence. Ryan stood in the doorway, half in half out, his expression as horrified as she knew her own must be.

Her mind devoid of any coherent thought, Hilary panicked. Scooting down the side-aisle, she ducked past him and out of the shop, where she continued to run blindly until she was caught up against a solid chest.

'What?' Leo demanded as he wrenched back to stare down into her almost terror-stricken face. 'What, Hilary?' he grated roughly as he gave her a little shake.

'Ryan,' she croaked.

'Where?'

'In the shop.'

'Right,' he said shortly. Turning her round, he began propelling her back the way she'd come.

'No!' she exclaimed in horror. Digging in her heels, she refused to move. 'No, Leo!'

'Yes,' he argued grimly. Gone was the amiable giant; his face now was totally transformed. He looked suddenly very tough and dangerous. 'You're going to go in and face him. Yes, you are!' he repeated as she fervently shook her head.

'I can't,' she whispered. 'Truly, Leo, I can't.'

Dragging her round to face him, he framed her desolate face with warm palms. 'You've been sitting in that damned cottage for nigh on a year and you've become a coward. He's a thief, Hilary,' he grated almost savagely. 'If someone broke into your house and you caught him, you'd beat him over the head, wouldn't you?'

'Would I?' she asked helplessly, not sure she'd do anything of the sort.

'Yes, you would. So you will walk into that store and give him the haughtiest stare you are capable of—and you can do it,' he promised. 'You can look like the most arrogant duchess when you choose. I know—I've had it turned on me! So stop bleating that you can't! You can! And, if I have to drag you there, you are going to do it!'

'But why is he here?' she wailed.

'I don't know. I'll ask him.'

'You can't!' she exclaimed in horror.

'Of course I can! If you want to know something, you ask. Very forthright lot, we Aussies,' he added with a grin that wasn't amiable at all.

Staring up at him, searching his eyes, she knew he was right, only there suddenly seemed a very large gap between knowing it and doing it. The Hilary of once upon a time would have done it and taken great pleasure in confronting him, but the Hilary of now seemed to have become a spineless coward. The mere thought of facing Ryan again made her feel sick. 'But what shall I say?'

'Nothing,' he said succinctly. 'Absolutely nothing. If he attempts to talk to you, you will flick him a haughty glance and say nothing. Now, stop wasting time.'

Total panic clenching her insides, her mind squirrelling uselessly, she allowed Leo to urge her back towards the shop. When they reached the door she hesitated and threw him a pleading look.

With a faint smile, he pushed the door wide and, knowing very well that as soon as the bell was heard all would look towards the door, kissed her. A hard, swift kiss that robbed her of thought entirely.

Her cheeks pink, she took a deep breath, and, enormously grateful for the solid bulk of Leo at her back, she stepped inside.

'Silly girl walked off with my car-keys,' Leo lied, giving an acceptable excuse for her sudden dash out of the shop. 'The Land Rover's kaput,' he elaborated.

No one would believe his fiction, but at least it was something they could all pretend to accept.

Taking his cue from Leo, Frank Green went one better. 'Wife did that,' he said laconically. 'Took the car into the garage and the silly cow went off with the keys. Took me ages to track her down. Now,' he continued, giving Hilary a warm smile, 'it was paint you wanted, wasn't it? I'd suggest matt vinyl. . .' And after that they all took over, shielding Hilary from Ryan, who was standing to one side, being comprehensively ignored.

After one quick glance at him, Hilary kept her back turned. She felt an almost hysterical desire to scream at them all. Only she didn't, but without Leo's heavy arm round her shoulders she thought she might have run out again.

Gazing blankly at the colour chart that was thrust into her hands, she felt as though she was falling apart at the seams, as though all the muscles and tendons that were holding her body together were snapping one by one. Allowing the babble of forced conversation to wash over her, she looked up at Leo. He was talking and smiling as though nothing in the world were different, yet the expression in his eyes belied his easy manner. He looked like a man waiting for something. A man possessed of infinite patience.

Unable to bear the tension any longer, she turned to look at Ryan. It was a face most women would find attractive, she supposed, capable of great charm. The soft fair hair and blue eyes that could be so disarming. At the moment his mouth was twisted with anger, and that made it easier, Hilary thought. Giving him a look of contempt that took almost all of her small store of courage, she turned back to Frank

Green. 'White, would you think?' she asked, her voice a high squeak, then let her breath out in an explosion of relief as she heard the shop door open and close.

'Has he gone?' she whispered.

'Yes,' Frank said in satisfaction.

'Would you excuse me for a moment?' Leo asked. 'I ought to get these keys to the garage.' Giving Hilary's shoulder a reassuring squeeze, he added, 'And don't go trying to carry that paint home alone. Wait here for me. I won't be long.'

As the door closed behind him, Hilary gazed back at the paint chart, feeling abandoned and lost. She knew where he was going—to confront Ryan, and she didn't want him to. As she made a move as though to go after him, Frank said easily, 'Do as he says, lass; leave Leo to sort it out. He's more than capable, I reckon.'

Staring at him, then round at the circle of concerned faces, she whispered, 'I don't want there to be any trouble.'

'There won't be,' Frank assured her.

'But why did he come back?' she asked helplessly.

'To find out why he couldn't get planning permission, I expect,' Frank answered almost gleefully. 'Every time he applies it gets turned down, on one pretext or another. My brother's on the council,' he explained. Seeing that Hilary wasn't taking it in, he added, 'Ryan and his

partner thought they'd easily get planning permission to build an estate on the land where
your cottage stood. Only he didn't reckon on
the villagers. Even if he hadn't cheated you,
which would have been more than enough on
its own to make us put a stop to his plans, we
certainly don't intend to have a housing estate.
Not here, we don't. This is a small village, old-
fashioned maybe, a bit feudal in some respects,
but we like it. Wouldn't stay here if we didn't
would we? So we set about putting a stop to it.
The colonel knew all the right people to
approach, and every time Ryan submits the
plans they put a stop to them. Thought he'd
make a killing, you see; a lot of money to be
made from property development.'

'So Ryan's stuck with a piece of land he can't
develop and can only sell as it stands at market
value?' she asked, beginning to enjoy the irony
of it.

'Which is very little more than he paid for it.
It won't get you your money back for you, love,
but it was the best we could think of.'

'I see. And you think that's why he came? To
find out?'

'I reckon. Didn't expect you to be here,
though, did he? That gave him a bit of a jolt.'

'And nor would I,' she said slowly, 'if you
hadn't all been so kind.'

'Well, we couldn't stand by, now, could we?
Ryan was one of our own, you might say, came
from the village, so it was up to us to try and

put it right. Make amends in the only way we could. Find you somewhere to stay, somewhere you could lick your wounds in private; somewhere we could keep an eye, so to speak, make sure you were all right.'

'And just as you was coming out of it, going to paint the cottage and all, the bastard comes back! Strewth!' Mrs Beeson expostulated, astonishing not only Hilary, but everyone else as well. Mrs Beeson was not normally given to strong language; most certainly not in a loud voice—and most certainly not in an Australian accent!

'I don't know what to say,' Hilary whispered, a hard painful lump in her throat. It had never even occurred to her to wonder why the land where the cottage had stood was still empty. She never went past that way if she could possibly avoid it.

'Then don't say anything,' Frank said with a grin. 'Besides, we like you, even if you are a foreigner. It works both ways, you know. We do for you, you do for us.'

'But I haven't done anything—except be an absolute misery,' she added honestly as she realised for perhaps the first time what a wet blanket she had been. In London you could be robbed, mugged, murdered, even, and no one would take the blindest bit of notice, yet here, in this little backwater, they'd done all they could and more. She had sometimes longed for the anonymity of London, and now felt doubly guilty for the thought. Ashamed.

'Think we don't know about the carvings you do for the hospital?' he asked, then smiled at her look of astonishment. 'It's a small community, Hilary, and the hospital is part of it. Dr Johannsen told us all about the work you do, about how you wouldn't take payment for it, and you so hard up and all. So, as I said, it works both ways. Now,' he continued, his voice brisk, 'paint. Don't think white would be suitable—too stark. Cream, maybe. . .magnolia; go better with the old beams. Need two, maybe three coats; couple of litres should do it. Got a tray? Roller? Brushes?'

Shaking her head, she watched the growing pile of equipment on the counter with dismay. She really didn't think she could afford all that. She'd only intended to buy a small tin of paint and one brush. 'How much do I owe you?' she asked weakly.

'Put it on the account.'

'But I don't have an account,' she protested.

'You do now. You just wait there for Leo,' he said kindly. 'I don't suppose he'll be long. Now then, ladies,' he continued sternly as he turned to the others, 'this isn't a social club; what will you all be wanting?'

Feeling a bit like a mechanical doll that couldn't function without a key, Hilary meekly stood to one side. Her life didn't seem to be anything to do with herself any more. Everyone else seemed to have the directing of it. The colonel, the village, even Leo. Did they all think her incapable of making her own decisions? Even the colour of the paint had been decided without her.

When the doorbell pinged, they all turned again like puppets operated by one grand master, nodding and smiling at each other as Leo came in.

'All ready?' he asked with a smile. Picking up her paint and other paraphernalia, he nodded at Frank, gave a general smile all round, and went out. Hastily following, turning to give them all a lame smile, she joined Leo on the pavement.

'Did you see him?'

'Of course,' he agreed amiably.

'Well, what did he say? '

'Not much,' he dismissed as he carried on walking towards the cottage.

'Leo!' she exclaimed crossly as she gave a little hop and a skip to keep up with his long strides. 'You're behaving as though nothing has happened!'

'Nothing has. I had a few words with him, then came back to the shop.'

'But what did you say?' she persisted.

Sighing, he came to a halt and leaned back against the hedge they were passing. Shifting her belongings more comfortably in his arms, he explained mildly, 'I told him that if he ever came within one hundred yards of you I'd break his neck. All right? Can we go now? These things are getting heavy.' Without waiting for her answer, he turned and ambled off, leaving Hilary standing with her mouth open.

Clamping her mouth shut, she stormed after him, suddenly furious that everyone was treating her like a child. 'Why are you taking this unwarranted interest in my affairs?' she demanded. 'The whole damned village has entered into a conspiracy to protect me! I'm not a baby, you know!'

'Yes, you are,' he said quietly. 'You obviously haven't got the first idea when it comes to a relationship. . . Oh, here comes the Land Rover,' he added, all in the same breath. Practically sprinting the last few yards to the cottage, he pushed inside and dumped her belongings on the kitchen table before dashing out again and after the Land Rover as it groaned and grunted its way up the track to the colonel's house, presumably driven by the garage mechanic.

'Well, really!' You will count very slowly to ten, Hilary admonished herself as she stood in the lane watching Leo's rapidly diminishing figure. You will not scream and throw a tantrum. You will walk very carefully into the cottage, you will put the kettle on and make some tea.

Doing as she had bid herself, she walked into the cottage and then spoilt it all by slamming the door. She didn't think she had ever met a man who so infuriated her. A man who was so evasive, so totally uncaring of anyone's feelings—and what the hell had he meant about a relationship? Just because she'd made one mistake. . . All right, so she'd been a bit odd since Ryan had left. All right, so she'd been a misery and hermit-like—wasn't she entitled to be? What did everyone expect, for goodness' sake? Rapture?

Needing an outlet for her gathering frustration, she collected the bulbs she had bought in Norwich earlier in the week and took them out into the little garden. She rummaged in the shed for the fork and emerged even more tousled and grumpy to spike it into the ground with the wish that it was Leo's indifferent back!

Being in a temper was certainly very good for the garden. It took her no time at all to turn over the bed along by the rickety fence. Collecting the trowel, she bent down and began stabbing it into the bigger clumps of earth to break them up. As she muttered to herself about interfering Australians who couldn't mind their own business she didn't hear Leo come back, or see him loom over the fence. In fact, she had no premonition that he was there at all until he spoke.

'Bit late for planting bulbs, isn't it?' he enquired pleasantly.

With a little start, she looked up and glared at him. 'Go away,' she snapped.

'Tsk, tsk, temper, temper. I only came to ask what you thought when you saw him again.'

'Oh, did you?' she asked derisively as she got

to her feet. 'Full of tact and finesse, aren't you? What the hell did you expect me to feel? Joy? Shocked was how I felt. Much as I feel now at your damned silly question! Go away, Leo; go and play with the Land Rover—I feel sure it will present more of a challenge than I will.'

'Didn't you feel desire? Want? Need?' he persisted mildly as he folded his arms along the fence and rested his chin on top.

'I don't believe you,' she muttered faintly. 'I really don't believe that even you could be so insensitive. Even if it had anything to do with you, which it doesn't.'

'True,' he admitted blandly, seemingly in no way embarrassed or offended by her tone. 'But the colonel said I wasn't to leave you here to brood.'

'I am not brooding, dammit! I am trying to plant bulbs!'

'And what if he comes over now? What if he just walks along the lane?'

'I don't know!' she gritted. Clencing her teeth until her jaw ached, she gave him a baleful stare while she wondered if she actually had the courage to hit him with the trowel. 'I'll cope, I expect, I've coped for the past year. . .'

'Existed,' he put in helpfully.

'All right! Existed!' she shouted. 'What the hell was I supposed to do? Just forget it? Pretend it never happened?'

'Fight back,' he said positively. Walking round the end of the fence, he came to stand beside her. 'Stop being such a damned little ostrich. Now——'

'Leo, she said warningly, 'I have had as much as I intend taking for one day. Will you please go away? Go and see your sister, your nephew——'

'No. I——'

'Just don't come and annoy me,' she continued firmly, overriding his interruption. 'I do not need your spurious concern—and, anyway, I don't expect he'll come back.'

'Oh, he will,' he insisted, smiling rather nastily at her. 'I guarantee it. He wants to know why you're still here.'

'I'm beginning to wonder that myself!' she exclaimed weakly. 'I really am. All I wanted was a tin of paint. It's not so much to ask, is it? A tin of paint? And since when have you been such an excellent student of human nature? How can you possibly know what he will do?'

'Because I've just seen him making his way in this direction,' he concluded triumphantly.

Her shoulders slumping tiredly, she leaned against the fork handle. 'Terrific.' Glancing at him, she queried helplessly, 'Do you ever have days when you wish you'd stayed in bed?'

'Certainly. And if you were in it with me, I wouldn't want to get out at all,' he said outrageously.

'Leo!'

'What?' he asked innocently, as a slow smile transformed his face.

She didn't answer, for the simple reason that she couldn't think of anything to say because the smile he had given her had been so totally unlike any other he had turned in her direction, so warm, and devastating, crinkling his eyes. . .

'Stand on the fork,' he instructed softly.

'I beg your pardon?' she queried blankly.

'Stand on the fork,' he repeated. 'You're too short, Ryan won't be able to see you above the fence unless you do.'

'Why should I want Ryan to see me?' she asked faintly.

'Because we are going to pay him back.'

'We are? How?'

'When he walks round the corner, he is going to see you being very thoroughly kissed. By me.'

'Oh, no. Oh, no, Leo,' she denied hastily as she tried to back away, her expression clearly indicative of her alarm.

'Yes,' he contradicted softly.

'No. Leo!' she exclaimed in shock as he caught hold of her and manoeuvred her back towards the fork. 'He doesn't like me! He won't care tuppence if he sees another man kissing me!' And the thought of Leo actually kissing her properly made her feel positively ill! Which was a thought she didn't want to stop and analyse.

'Oh, yes, he will,' he insisted. 'Men like Ryan always mind. There's a rather weird psychology to people like that. You were his victim; he wants it to stay that way. Believe me, sweetheart, bastards like that will always mind. Hurts their notion of pride, you see. Not only that,' he continued, his eyes steady on hers, 'but when he sees that another man wants you he'll begin to wonder what he missed. He wrote you off, you see; now he'll have second thoughts.'

'Oh, I see; it's two of a kind, is it? You know how he'll behave because you'd behave the same,' she sneered scathingly, then yelped in alarm when he curved a large hand round her neck and urged her roughly towards him, giving Hilary little choice but to climb on to the fork. Staring at his obdurate face, she pleaded helplessly, 'Leo, please don't do this. He won't care, despite your amateur psychology. Truly he won't. Anyway, I don't want to see him,' she added sulkily.

'Then shut your eyes,' he told her indifferently. 'Now, put your arms round my neck. Do it!' he commanded. He sounded so utterly unlike the Leo she thought she was used to that she automatically obeyed.

Gazing into eyes that were suddenly like warm velvet, she swallowed drily as an unbearable excitement flooded her. She didn't even stop to wonder why the thought of confronting Ryan again hardly bothered her. Placing her arms loosely round Leo's neck, she gave a little grunt of pain when the fork handle that was between them pressed into her ribs.

'Bit like a chastity belt, isn't it?' he commented with amusement. 'Ready?'

'I suppose,' she decided, even as she wondered why on earth she was even considering his plan, 'but I feel extremely silly.' And shivery, she mentally added, and hungry for him.

'Oh, ye of little faith,' he taunted. 'Within half a second of my mouth touching yours, I guarantee that all thoughts of Ryan will fly out of your head.'

Which was precisely what was troubling her. It might be a whole lot safer to keep thoughts of Ryan very firmly in her head. With some half-formed idea of remonstrating with him all over again, she began hesitantly. 'Leo——'

'Hush. Most men with a modicum of experience can make a woman feel special, you know,' he murmured soothingly.

'And you, no doubt, have more than a modicum!' she snapped, infuriated by his bland arrogance.

'Of course,' he agreed with a wide grin. His eyes searching hers from very close quarters, he chuckled when she hastily lowered her lashes. Placing warm palms against her shoulder-blades, he blew gently on her closed lips, and her eyes flew open in surprise. 'Open your mouth,' he ordered softly.

'Why?' she croaked.

'Because it's better that way,' he commented mildly as though surprised at her slowness.

'Leo! It's only a demonstration! Not for real!'

'Says who? Did I ever say anything about a demonstration?'

'You said. . .' she began weakly.

'I know what I said. Now, open your mouth—not wide!' he reproved, giving her a little shake.

Taking a deep breath, as though she were about to plunge into deep water, which successfully parted her mouth, she had her exhaling breath cut off as his mouth touched hers, parting it even further, and a delicious shiver of pleasure went down her spine. Helpless in the grip of emotions that refused to be denied, she finally admitted to herself that it was what she wanted; what she had wanted since he had kissed her, oh, so gently, in the kitchen. His mouth was warm and dry, and very experienced, and with a sigh of pleasure she relaxed against him. As his mouth moved sensuously on hers, she tightened her arms round his neck and slid her fingers into the thick hair at the nape, then stiffened in shock when his tongue intruded between her teeth. All sorts of alarming sensations rioting in the pit of her stomach, she mumbled incoherently against his mouth as she tried to arch closer, only to be thwarted by the fork handle. She wanted to touch her body to his, feel his powerful thighs against her own. Wanted him with an urgency and desperation that shocked her. She had allowed him to dictate what happened, yet now she wanted more. Vaguely ashamed of her behaviour, she then tried to draw back, but his arms tightened, preventing her, and she gave up all thoughts of resistance.

Exchanging small, urgent, drugging kisses with him, she touched his mouth, his chin, nose, eyes, her breath coming in short gasps. As she moved her thumbs to the sensitive muscles where his neck and shoulders joined, she exerted gentle pressure, and warmth flooded through her when he groaned.

'Whose damned silly idea was it to use the fork?' he asked thickly. Lifting her bodily from it, he scooped her up into his arms and carried her into the cottage. Kicking open the living-room door, his mouth still firmly attached to hers, he sat in the armchair, her slim form cradled on his lap.

Wriggling closer, she slid her hands inside his shirt, which had somehow become unbuttoned, then shivered and held her breath as his warm palms roved beneath her sweater, and an almost physical pain exploded inside her as one thumb touched her nipple. Incoherent little sounds issuing from her arched throat, she moved her own hand to cover his. Pressing it more firmly against her breast as his breathing became as erratic as her own, she moved her mouth from his and buried her face in his neck.

'Oh, God, Leo. . .'

'Don't talk,' he instructed huskily, 'Just hang on tight and, for God's sake, keep still.'

'I am. . .'

'No, you aren't,' he denied thickly. 'You keep wriggling—and, oh, Hilly, I'm only human, and if you don't lie still there's going to be a very embarrassing incident.'

Lying rigid, her cheeks burning, she wanted to tell him it was all right, that she wanted him too. He wasn't the only one who ached. The feel of him against her set up so many conflicting emotions, as though there was a war raging inside her, and the only way to stop it was to give in to her needs, assuage the ache in her body. The effort to remain rigid was making her body quiver and she groaned against his neck, 'Make love to me. . .'

'Ah, don't,' he said gently. Removing his hand with marked reluctance from the warm swell of her breast, he straightened her jumper and smoothed the tangled hair away from her face. His eyes were a deep, dark grey, almost drugged, she saw as he turned her face up to his, and she guessed her own face must reflect the same emotions. With a deep, shaky breath, he gave her a lopsided smile that she found utterly endearing. 'There's nothing on this earth that I want more than to make love to you, but, if I do, later you'll regret it.'

'No, I won't,' she denied almost inaudibly.

'Yes. Right at this moment I've awakened needs you thought you'd buried, but in the cold light of morning you'll blame me for taking advantage.'

'No. . .'

'Yes,' he contradicted gently. 'So, just sit quiet

for a moment, there's a good girl, and then I'll make us a cup of tea.'

'Oh, Leo,' she laughed shakily, 'I don't want a cup of tea. I want to touch you, hold you, make love to you.'

'You think I don't?' he asked, and his voice seemed to shake with the effort to control it. Pushing his hand gently into her soft hair, he traced the perfect curve of her mouth with his thumb before murmuring throatily. 'I want to make love to you till your body is drugged with sensations, every nerve-ending alive, limbs warm and aching, mouth swollen from my kisses and your eyes a deep, dark purple. I want to touch you the way no man has ever touched you. I want you to touch me, trail your mouth from my toes to my eyes. I've wanted it for a very long time, and it will happen, I promise, but not now, not yet.'

'Why?' she pleaded.

'Because. . .' Letting his breath out on a long sigh, he changed his mind. Instead of explaining, he begged, 'Trust me, Hilary. Please?' When she gave a reluctant nod, he continued more briskly, 'Now I'll go and make the tea.' Standing, and slowly lowering her to stand on her own two feet, he stared down into her bewildered face before dropping a hard, swift kiss on her mouth. He released her abruptly and turned and walked into the kitchen.

CHAPTER FOUR

STARING blankly after Leo, Hilary tried to come to terms with what had happened. Ryan had never, ever made her feel like that, a quivering mass of frustration, had never produced this pain in her lower abdomen. Taking a deep, shaky breath, she slowly followed Leo. He was standing with his back to her, hands pressed flat on the kitchen table, and he was dragging deep breaths into his lungs.

Moving silently up behind him, she hesitantly touched his back and was quite unprepared for the violent start he gave.

'Leo?' she whispered.

When he swung round she stared at him helplessly, shocked by his appearance. He looked ravaged. Her own body felt as though it was burning up with fever, and she put out an unsteady hand to touch his face. 'Oh, Leo,' she whispered.

Dragging her into his arms, he pressed his mouth against her neck. 'I want you,' he muttered thickly. 'I want to take you violently, with passion! I don't want a complacent little doll that I can manipulate,' he said strangely, 'I want to fight for every damned caress—and I think I'm going insane. Shocked?'

'No,' she denied numbly, a hectic flush along her cheekbones, because she had just discovered that she also needed a man she could fight with, cross swords with. Ryan had never argued, never shouted back when she was being impossible; he'd just sulked and stormed out,— and there was no fun in that. Despite the constant friction with Leo, he made her feel gloriously alive. No man had ever said such things to her, but she certainly wasn't shocked. 'Excited,' she whispered, her voice a mere thread of sound.

'We should talk; there are things I should explain. . .'

'But not now,' she breathed as her eyes moved to his mouth. Taking a shaky little breath, she lifted her hand and traced her finger along the outline.

'No,' he agreed softly, 'not now.' He picked her up and carried her upstairs. Standing her beside the bed, his hands rough in their urgency, he began to undress her. As he moved her hands to his belt he commanded, 'Now undress me.'

Feeling so totally unlike her normal self, as though she was mesmerised, Hilary slowly removed his clothes. An unbearable feeling of excitement and need was building inside her, like bubbling lava, and she pressed warm, feverish kisses to his flesh. When she bent to tug his clothing from his feet, she leaned her head against him; then, unable to resist the temptation, she trailed her tongue along his hard-muscled thighs.

'Dear God, Hilary,' he gasped on a swiftly indrawn breath, 'don't do that.'

Halting, she sat back on her heels and just stared at him. Never before had she been so aware of a man's nakedness, of the beauty in a man's strong, well-proportioned frame. Ryan had never stood naked before her, never evinced any pride or unashamed arrogance in his appearance, but then Ryan had never really wanted her. Scrambling to her feet, she pressed herself to Leo, needing the reassurance of his strong arms.

Clasping her to him, he urged her off balance, his mouth claiming hers as they fell backwards across the narrow bed. His body, as though accustomed to her shape, her rhythm, accommodated itself to hers in perfect match.

She wasn't passive, didn't want to be, and as her fingers dug spasmodically into his back, finding each nerve-centre, then down to the base of his spine, she arched into him, her legs wrapped round his thighs, her head thrown back. Every part of her felt open to him, wanting him, needing the fulfilment only he could give. She was unaware of the words she uttered, the encouragement; was only aware of his hard male body, warm and competent on hers, the driving thrust that pushed her further and further away from reality. The room, the cottage,

Ryan, her lack of confidence, all faded; there was only now, this one moment in time, and nothing in her life had ever prepared her for the feelings she experienced. With one last cry she held him impossibly tight, her nails scoring his back, and knew even in her state of mindlessness that Leo had timed himself to her, that even in the grip of his own needs he had thought of her.

When he slumped against her, his flesh warm and damp, Hilary dragged long, deep breaths into her depleted lungs, her heart racing. For a moment she felt totally disorientated, lost, until his arms tightened round her and he lifted her head.

'Oh, Hilly, Hilly,' he breathed—and then he smiled, a beautiful, slow lopsided smile that made her heart turn over. 'If I have nothing else on this earth,' he continued quietly, 'I won't care. I think that was something that most people never achieve in a lifetime—and I feel quite ecstatically kn. . .tired,' he substituted with a grin.

Pushing the damp hair off his forehead with a hand that refused to keep still, she managed a shaky smile in response. 'I didn't know it could be like that,' she whispered.

'No, nor I. I thought it was only in dreams. And in daylight too,' he teased as though he could read her mind and know that never before had she been so uninhibited.

'Oh, Leo,' she exclaimed on a husky little

laugh, 'I can't believe this is happening! Yesterday you were arch enemy number one. . .'

'And now?' he asked softly.

'And now you're a magic carpet that can take me to paradise,' she said, not feeling in the least foolish for saying something so idiotic.

'Oh, Hilly,' he said again. Bending his head, he parted her mouth with soft insistence and rubbed his lips erotically against hers.

Feeling her body respond again, she slowly rolled him on to his back. As she stared down at him, her eyes huge, deep and dark, her hair tumbled wildly round her face, she gave a slow smile and began to trail provocative kisses from his nose, cheeks and eyes to his chin. Then with a little grin, so much like the old devil-may-care Hilary, she proceeded to demonstrate all her new-found skills, her hands and tongue touching every magnificent inch of him until he pleaded for her to stop.

'Can't take it, huh?' she teased, then yelped and began laughing helplessly as he yanked her up and rolled to hold her captive beneath him.

'Witch,' he told her, his face relaxed, boyish, showing the easy charm that she had not known he possessed while they had been so busy provoking each other. As he kissed and caressed her in turn, Hilary didn't think she had ever felt so happy or relaxed—well, relaxed until his mouth roved below her navel.

'Oh, God, Leo, no,' she gasped.

'Oh, God, Hilly, yes!' he laughed, and proceeded to demonstrate very ably that if she
thought she had experienced all there was to
experience she was sadly mistaken. When he
finally moved back to lie beside her, he pulled
her into his arms so that her head came to rest
on his chest. With one hand smoothing her
unruly hair, and the other resting on her hip, he
gave a long sigh of contentment.

Her own hand tracing the ridge of his breast-
bone, she found it almost impossible to compre-
hend that she was lying here naked with a man
she barely knew, and yet she was positively
revelling in the feel of warm masculine flesh,
the steady rise and fall of his chest.

'Tell me about you,' she instructed softly as
she moved her hand with slow enjoyment
across his flat stomach.

'Tell you what?' he asked as he hastily
clamped her hand still and moved it back to his
chest.

Raising her head to look at him, she gave him
a little slap. 'You know all about me, yet you
seem curiously reluctant to talk about yourself.'

'Mm,' he murmured ruefully, 'talkies time.'
As he raised her hand towards his mouth his
grey eyes widened, then gleamed with laughter
as he saw the state it was in. 'Good grief,
woman.'

Staring at her filthy hand, the mud-encrusted
nails, she burst out laughing. 'How terribly

unhygienic,' she gurgled. 'But it's your own
fault; you shouldn't have been so. . .'

'Ardent?' he asked helpfully, and it wasn't
much later that Hilary realised how skilfully
she'd been diverted. But now, staring in horrified fascination at her dirty hands, she pulled a
little face. 'I'd best go and have a wash.'

'Later,' he said positively as he pulled her
back into his arms. 'If you've infected me
already a few more minutes won't make much
difference,' then grunted with laughter when
she hit him. 'What a very violent girl you are.
Always walloping me.'

'You deserve it,' she said unrepentantly. 'You
probably weren't smacked enough as a child.
Well, go on, then, let's have all these dark and
sordid secrets, the result, no doubt, of a misspent youth.'

'Misspent?' he exclaimed. 'Let me tell you, I
never had time to misbehave. Up at dawn,
rolling, exhausted, into bed at dusk. . .'

'Down the opal mines, were we?' she teased
as she leaned up to look down into his humorous face.

'Not quite. Sheep station, and sheep don't all
stand tidily together, you know, waiting to be
tended. They wander. Very stupid animals,
sheep. Then there's the dipping, shearing,
round-ups,   then   there's   the   damned
paperwork. . .'

'Oh, my heart bleeds,' she quipped, her eyes
full of laughter. Unable to resist the lovely

temptation to touch him, she traced her finger over his features before combing the fall of dark hair back off his forehead, her fingers lingering in the silky strands. 'Wear a hat with corks, did you?' she teased naughtily.

'No, I did not wear a hat with corks!' he refuted disgustedly. 'Why do all foreigners think we wear those damned silly hats with corks?'

'Well, some do,' she murmured. 'I've seen pictures. And is that what you still do? Oh, no,' she corrected herself as she remembered one of their earlier conversations, 'I forgot—you're in property. Sheep get too much for you?'

'No, I——' Breaking off, he frowned as the sound of urgent tooting came from outside. 'What the hell. . .?'

Scrambling to her knees, Hilary peered through the window. 'There's a cream car in the lane,' she explained, 'and the driver is standing beside it and leaning on the horn.'

'The hire car. Oh, hell, I'd forgotten all about it.' Extricating himself with some difficulty from the tangled bedclothes, Leo continued, 'I'll have to go.' Swiftly dragging on his clothes, he pressed a swift kiss on her startled mouth. With his unbuttoned shirt hanging outside his trousers, and his bare feet thrust into his shoes, he clattered out and down the stairs, his socks clutched ridiculously in his hand.

Watching from the window, Hilary grinned as she saw him hurry towards the driver, and only when he'd climbed into the car did she move.

Lying back down on the rumpled bed, she stretched luxuriously, then hooked her hands round the bed-head and stared up at the ceiling, a soft smile on her face. Would he come back? He hadn't actually said he would—but then, neither had he said he wouldn't.

Feeling suddenly full of energy, she got up, and, switching on the immersion heater so that she could have a bath later, she decided to give the cottage a good clean. It was a bit late to start her painting; she'd do that tomorrow, she decided.

By the time she'd thoroughly cleaned the cottage, had her bath and something to eat, it was gone ten, and Hilary finally admitted to herself that Leo wasn't coming back. Had she been a complete fool? she wondered. Standing at the kitchen window, she stared out into the garden. She could just make out the shape of the fork stuck in the ground, the bulbs scattered around as she had left them, and as the moon disappeared behind the clouds she shivered and a feeling of desolation flooded over her. Now that she was thinking more rationally, all the old doubts came back, and she found it hard to believe that she could have behaved so rashly. It was she who had begged him to make love to her, she recalled, not the other way round, and, although he hadn't been exactly reluctant, what man was going to turn down such a blatant offer? She didn't even understand why she didn't feel ashamed.

Finally deciding it was not only pointless, but spineless as well to stand at the door waiting for a man who wouldn't come, she went up to bed, and surprisingly she fell asleep almost at once, only to be woken some hours later by a violent storm. As the thunder growled menacingly overhead and lightning forked the sky in a glorious display of pyrotechnics, Hilary burrowed her head back under the covers, but dragged it reluctantly out again as she became aware of the rather ominous sound of dripping water.

It was difficult to be absolutely sure, but over and above the sound of the torrential downpour outside she was sure she could detect the steady drip of water from inside. Peering at the little bedside clock, she groaned. It was only five o'clock. Slumping back on the pillow, she tried to ignore it. Closing her eyes, she listened to the soft rumble of thunder, more distant this time, and the persistent plop, plip, plop of dripping water that unfortuantely wasn't in the least distant. As she strained her ears, trying to pinpoint its exact location, she gave an exclamation of disgust and thrust the duvet aside. It wasn't going to go away on its own, was it? And if she left it, God alone knew what sort of mess there would be in the morning.

Shivering in the chilly air, she groped across to the light switch. Not totally sure she actually wanted to illuminate what she already knew she was going to find, she snapped down the switch and stared disagreeably at the glistening drops that plopped relentlessly on to the dresser.

'Oh, knickers.'

She hurried back to the bed and snatched up her dressing-gown, and as she shrugged into it she saw the note that was carefully pinned to the pillow. Grabbing it with a hand that shook, she slowly opened it up. It was written on the back of the paint bill from the shop, and she had a sudden vision of Leo hunting frantically round in the dark for something to write on. A small sad smile pulling at her mouth, convinced that it would say thank you and goodbye, she took a deep breath, and began to read. 'You looked too lovely to wake, so I didn't. I'll see you in the morning—and, in future, lock your back door! Love, Leo.'

Love? she mused, and she didn't think she quite liked the idea of Leo watching her while she slept. Quite why she didn't like it, she wasn't sure, but then, she wasn't sure of anything very much where Leo was concerned. But he must like her a bit, mustn't he? If he'd come back? With a silly smile on her face she walked across to stare at her reflection in the dressing-table mirror. You're twenty-seven, she told her image in an attempt to instil some common sense into it. A supposedly confident, mature woman. Accept his lovemaking as a special gift and don't read more into it than there is. No.

Right. With a firm little nod, and still smiling, she pushed the note into her dressing-gown pocket before going downstairs to find a bucket.

Yawning widely, the bucket held in her arms, she climbed back upstairs. Standing it on top of the dresser to catch the drips, she instructed it firmly, 'Don't fill up before morning.' Flinging off her dressing-gown, she climbed back into the now cold bed and snuggled beneath the covers. She knew exactly what it was, of course, she thought sleepily. The guttering that she had bodged up a few months previously had come loose again. Well it would have to be another bodge up; she couldn't afford to get a builder in.

As she turned over on to her back she dismissed such mundane things as guttering and went over the words on Leo's note. 'Love, Leo,' meant nothing at all, she tried to convince herself. It was just a casual phrase that was tossed back and forth between acquaintances, and meant nothing—only she didn't want it to mean nothing. Closing her eyes, she tried to regain sleep that had never seemed more elusive. She conjured up an image of a five-barred gate, introduced some jumping sheep and attempted to count them, then giggled when they appeared wearing cork-strewn hats.

Giving up on the sheep, she stared at the curtain that fluttered in the cool breeze through the ill-fitting window and tried to recapture the warmth and pleasure of their lovemaking, the feel of his body moving with hers, but was

unable to shut out the infuriating sound of the
steady drip into the bucket like Chinese water-
torture. She tried wrapping the pillow round
her ears; tried mind over matter; tried burrowing
under the duvet, and then gave up. With a cross
little sound in the back of her throat, she irritably
kicked the covers aside. Resigned to the fact that
she wasn't going to get back to sleep, she pulled
on her robe and went downstairs. Maybe a cup
of tea would help.

While waiting for the kettle to boil, she stood
at the window watching the rain. It was absolutely pouring down as though someone up top
was emptying buckets. It pounded the soft earth
and gurgled along the gutters to splash with
relentless monotony into the tub outside the
back door. A steady splat, splat, splat that was
extremely irritating. After making the tea she sat
at the kitchen table to drink it, and was still
sitting there when dawn broke. As the rain
gradually died away, birds began to fight and
squabble like fractious children just allowed out
after being cooped up indoors; but then they
didn't have leaky roofs; neither did they have to
climb up there as soon as it was light to inspect
the damage; or have a meeting with Leo, the
thought of which made her feel weak inside.
She wasn't naïve enough to think he was in love
with her; nor did she think she was in love with
him—or not very much—but the thought of
that strong body and craggy face, of grey eyes

that could be either icily remote or filled with humour, made her tremble.

Her elbows propped on the table, the cup still held between her palms, she watched the pale weak sun climb above the horizon and draw glistening prisms from rain-soaked hedgerows and grass, giving beauty to the flat landscape. Yawning widely, she put down her empty cup, pillowed her head on folded arms and drifted into a half-sleep that distorted reality, muffled outside sounds like the clink and rattle of the milk-float, a distant dog's barking, the choked cough of a car reluctant to start.

Waking with a jump, disorientated for a moment, Hilary stared in disbelief at the kitchen clock. It was gone nine. Oh, hell. So much for an early start. As she hurried upstairs to the bedroom, which still seemed to hold Leo's presence, she tried not to indulge in daydreams that would in all probability prove to be no more substantial than the rainbows she'd witnessed earlier. After a quick wash she dragged on an old pair of jeans and an equally ancient navy sweater before emptying the bucket and replacing it on the dresser. The plaster on the ceiling was already beginning to peel, and she scowled at it. 'Do you have to do these things to me?' But there was humour in her tone, and a sparkle in her lovely eyes, and the mouth that had been unhappy for so long now curved in a smile.

Collecting the ladder from the shed, she searched around for the claw hammer she'd

used before to slot the gutter back under the
tiles. After throwing things around in a very
haphazard fashion she finally abandoned her
search. Maybe the colonel would have one; she
didn't suppose he would mind if she borrowed
it. Hurrying up the lane, feeling absurdly
young, she hummed under her breath. It was
ridiculous to feel so happy, ridiculous to ignore
the cautionary voices inside her head, but she
couldn't help it. She'd been miserable too long,
yet she felt a sort of sick excitement at the
thought of meeting Leo.

There was no sign of him, nor the hire car,
and just for a moment her confidence faltered.
Had he not been as eager to see her as she him?
Telling herself not to be stupid, she went into
the barn. Unfortunately, it looked about as
efficiently laid out as her shed, with clutter and
rubbish strewn everywhere. Rummaging
around on the bench, she finally found a long
chisel which, she decided, would have to do.

Having walked back to the cottage, she put
the ladder against the wall, then tested it to
make sure it was firm. She stuffed the chisel in
her back pocket, climbed up, then stared in
surprise at the guttering. It didn't look to be in
the least loose. Prodding it experimentally, and
finding it quite firm, she looked up over the
roof. Two tiles had slipped. Damn. She prayed
the guttering would hold her weight as she
slowly hauled herself up until she could sit
astride the peak of the roof. And why was it,

she wondered, that, if tiles had to slip, it had to be the ones that were the most inaccessible? They couldn't be near the gutter or the peak; oh, no, they had to be halfway between. Muttering and grumbling to herself, she reached gingerly down.

'Need any help?' a mild voice asked from close behind her.

Nearly falling off the roof in fright, Hilary grabbed frantically at the chimney stack to keep her balance. She peered awkwardly over her shoulder at a very bland-looking Leo and snorted in exasperation. 'What are you trying to do? Kill me?'

'Sorry,' he apologised affably. Resting his elbows along the gutter as though it were some convenient garden fence and not at least twenty feet above the ground, he commented helpfully, 'You don't look very proficient, if I might say so.'

'No, you may not say so!' she exclaimed, yet was quite unable to hide the breathless excitement she felt at the sight at him. 'And, from someone who's just successfully ruined the gearbox of the Land Rover, that, if I might say so,' she parodied, 'is the height of impertinence. Do you know anything about roofs?'

His lips pursed thoughtfully, his eyes gleaming with laughter, he finally shook his head.

'No, I didn't think you did, so kindly go away and stop trying to put me off.'

'I was only trying to help.'

'Well, you aren't, you're hindering, so kindly go away.' Her eyes smiling, she continued with her repairs. He'd looked as though he was really pleased to see her, not awkward or evasive, and as he continued to watch her she hastily dragged her mind back to the matter in hand. Most men would have insisted on doing it themselves, and she was curiously grateful for his confidence in her ability. With a sigh of relief as the second tile slotted into place, she replaced the chisel in her back pocket and began to edge backwards until Leo could grasp her ankles and guide her feet to the top of the ladder.

'Thanks,' she said breathlessly. Expecting that he would now let her go and retreat down the ladder, she was startled when his large hands gripped her thighs and continued to guide her until she was standing two steps above him. Because of his superior height, his head was on a level with hers and she could feel his breath stirring her hair. With a little shiver, she muttered awkwardly, 'Well, go on, then, or are we going to stand on the ladder all day?'

'It has its recommendations,' he said softly against her ear, and his tongue gently touched the lobe.

Feeling weak and boneless, she reproved huskily, 'Oh, God, Leo, not on top of a ladder.'

'Why not?' he queried as his mouth moved to the cord in her neck, destroying what little command over her senses she had left. 'Very useful things, ladders, especially when you're on the top of one—there's nowhere for you to run, which I get the feeling you are contemplating, and I think even you aren't callous enough to push me off backwards.'

'Want to bet?' And what do you mean, even me?' she exclaimed in mock outrage. Momentarily forgetting where they were, she tried to swing round to face him and Leo was forced to grab the gutter to steady them.

'Careful! Now, turn round very, very slowly,' he instructed.

She swallowed drily and asked huskily, 'Why can't we go down the ladder this way?' God, it was ridiculous—she was beginning to feel like a sixteen-year-old!

'Because we aren't going down the ladder. Now, turn round.'

Cautiously doing as he said, she gasped as he gripped her ankles between his knees and leaned his full weight against her. As she stared into his strong face from very, very close quarters, she held his broad shoulder for balance. He was insane, she decided, her nose practically touching his; totally insane. What normal man would use the top of a ladder to hold a conversation?

'Good morning,' he said throatily as his eyes smiled warmly into her own.

'Good morning,' she said shakily, unable to look away.

'Regretting it?' he queried.

She shook her head and felt colour wash into

her cheeks as his eyes drifted slowly over her face in a very thorough appraisal that made her feel both weak and excited. Shutting her eyes, she then snapped them open again in panic as his mouth touched gently against hers. He wasn't holding her tight; her breasts barely touched against his chest, and only his powerful thighs touched hers, but that was quite enough, she discovered. Her breath fluttering jerkily in her chest, she whispered, 'Please don't, Leo. Please let me down.'

'What are you afraid of? I'm only going to kiss you. Once, very gently, very softly, very thoroughly.' His eyes holding hers in an almost hypnotic stare, he asked softly, 'What's so terrible about a kiss?'

'Nothing,' she croaked, 'but not on the top of a ladder.'

She might just as well have saved her breath, because he kissed her anyway. He didn't exactly force her mouth open; in fact, she wasn't quite sure how hers came to be parted. It wasn't a conscious move on her part, and yet, once open to his erotically roving tongue, she was helpless to do anything except melt against him with a low moan as the same desire as yesterday curled through her stomach. Feeling weightless and soft, she slid her arms further round him, her fingers pushing into his thick hair. As she pressed closer, Hilary shuddered slightly as their lower bodies came into contact. He wasn't unmoved either, and his slow arousal against

her made her arch into him. Feeling drugged
and quite incredibly wanton, she moved her
fingers to his jaw. She slid them softly to touch
his lower lip as he kissed her, and gasped when
he eased the pressure and bit gently against the
tip of one finger before recapturing her mouth
in a slow drugging kiss that seemed to go on
forever.

'I have to go out again,' he murmured against
her mouth. 'I'll only be about an hour—I hope.
Am I invited to lunch?'

Not sure that her voice would actually work,
she merely nodded.

'And we still have to talk,' he added, omin-
ously, Hilary felt. With a last swift kiss on her
parted mouth, he slid expertly down the ladder
and, as soon as she was safely down, he strode
off, whistling.

A hesitant hand to her mouth, a rather
bemused smile in her eyes, she watched him
walk away. She was still standing there when
he drove past in the rented car. Giving him a
foolish little wave, she decided she'd better
return the chisel before she forgot all about it.
With a little grin, she began trudging up the
lane.

Now, what should she get for lunch? Wine?
she wondered. No, that might look too—what?
Expectant? Celebratory? So, no wine. She'd go
to the shops, then have a bath, change into—
what? Most of her clothes were either tailored
for work or casual; when she was at home she

normally only wore jeans and sweaters, she thought, then gave a little laugh at her behaviour. It was also proving very hard not to read more into his behaviour than he might have meant. She'd been hurt once, very badly; she didn't want to lay herself open to that sort of pain again.

Returning the chisel to the bench, she turned to leave and came face to face with Leo's sister. Or who she assumed was his sister—they hadn't actually been introduced.

'Just returning the chisel,' she explained lamely. 'I borrowed it earlier.'

'Well, thank God for that!' the other girl exclaimed humorously. 'I thought you were a burglar! And if you had been I know just exactly who my brother would have blamed! Me!' Holding out her hand, she introduced herself. 'Gwen.'

'Hilary.'

'Hi,' Gwen said easily. 'Want some tea? I was just going to make some.'

'Oh, no, not really,' she disclaimed hastily, not sure she was ready for a tête-á-tête with Leo's sister. 'I only brought the chisel back.'

'Oh, come on, you've got time for a cup of tea, surely?' Using the same forthrightness as her brother, she took Hilary's arm in a firm grip and began walking back to the house.

Without being downright rude, Hilary couldn't think how to get out of it. Glancing sideways at her companion, she gave a resigned shrug. Gwen looked to be a couple of years older than herself, and, whereas Leo was dark, his sister was a redhead with green eyes, which looked as though they might be very astute, Hilary decided with sinking spirits. Her feelings for Leo were too new to bear cross-examination.

'You can't have seen much of your brother,' she commented, merely by way of conversation. She knew very well Gwen hadn't seen much of him—he was always in her cottage!

'No, I haven't, which is why I came over today! And that did me a lot of good, didn't it? The minute I arrived he rushed off. Do you know where he's gone?'

'No,' Hilary denied. Not wanting to give the impression that Leo might confide in her, she left it at that. Not that she did know where he'd gone; she didn't.

'Don't stand around,' Gwen said with a grin as they went into the kitchen. 'Sit down, tea won't be long. Neither, hopefully, will my dear brother. Honestly, he's driving me insane!' she exclaimed as she stirred the Aga into reluctant life.

Well, that makes two of us, Hilary thought with a little smile as she sat at the table. It was nice to know she wasn't the only one to suffer from his outrageous behaviour.

'Why he gets involved with other people's troubles, I'll never know,' she continued in happy ignorance that she was just about to put her foot in it. 'Just because he looks amiable—

which is the complete and utter misconception people are apt to labour under—people he barely knows ask him to do all sorts of weird and wonderful things. A couple he met quite recently—Nick, don't you dare come in here in those muddy boots!' she yelled, utterly confusing Hilary, who was still trying to digest the fact that Gwen thought Leo looked amiable. Hilary didn't think he looked amiable at all. Well, not mostly, she qualified to herself. Feeling heat suffuse her cheeks, she quickly turned her head away before Gwen could notice and stared straight into the brightly enquiring hazel eyes of a young boy. He looked to be about ten, his hair was as red as Gwen's, and his face was set in a horrible scowl.

Sounding for all the world as though she quite hated him, Gwen commented disgustedly, 'I have never known a child to get so dirty!'

'He's your son?' Hilary asked as she gave the boy a tentative smile.

'Yes, for my sins. So why have you come back?' she asked Nick. 'I though I told you to go out and play.'

'I'm hungry,' he complained.

'You're always hungry.'

Kicking off his muddy wellingtons, he came to stand beside Hilary. 'Hello,' he greeted her cheerfully, 'are you the one who's going to marry Uncle Matt?'

'Uncle Matt?' she queried blankly.

'Yeah. Oh, well, I guess if you don't know

who he is you can't be going to marry him, can
you?' he asked with irrefutable logic. Giving
Hilary a cheeky grin, he asked his mother, 'Can
I go down to the village?'

'If you must. Only don't be too long; if Matt's
not back in half an hour I'm going home.'

'OK.' Dragging his boots back on, he slammed
out.

'Honestly,' Gwen complained as she brought
two cups of tea over to the table and sat down,
'Matt's the only one who seems able to cope
with him. Even my husband is useless.
Now. . .'

'Is Matt your brother?' Hilary enquired
hesitantly.

'Yes, of course,' Gwen agreed, beginning to
look as confused as Hilary felt.

'Oh.' With a little laugh, she explained, 'I'm
sorry. I didn't realise there were two of them.'

'Two? Two what?'

'Brothers.'

'There aren't.' Frowning, she continued to
stare at Hilary in some perplexity. 'I've only got
one brother. Matt, Oh, my God.' Clapping her
hands together, she began to laugh delightedly.
'You haven't the faintest idea who Matt is, have
you?'

'No.'

Still grinning, she shook her head in self-
disgust. 'What an idiot you must think me. I
assumed you knew him. But what on earth
made you think there were two of them? Or no,

don't tell me,' she denied with a scowl every bit as horrible as her son's, 'he's adopted another blasted lame duck and has got him living here with him! Honestly, that man is the absolute limit!'

Staring at the other girl, her face puzzled, she began slowly, 'But Leo said——'

'Leo?' Her face magically clearing, Gwen exclaimed, 'But Leo is Matt! Good Lord, I haven't heard anyone call him that in years! Is that what he told you his name was?' When Hilary nodded confusedly, Gwen murmured thoughtfully, 'I wonder why.'

Which was exactly what Hilary was wondering. Was he being devious? Or did he just want a special name for her to use? Frowning, she looked down and began to idly trace intricate patterns on the table-top with her finger as she tried to puzzle it out. Suddenly recalling the boy's words, she froze and looked up, her face startled. When Gwen gave a rather knowing smile, she blushed scarlet. Before she would carry her thoughts to a satisfactory conclusion, Gwen was off again.

'I won't embarrass you by probing,' she said kindly. 'Now, where did I get to before Nick interrupted us? Oh, yes, this family in Port Headland. Can——'

'Port Headland?' Hilary queried faintly as her attention was violently captured.

'Yes. It's in Australia. North-west,' Gwen explained somewhat impatiently. 'Can you believe it?' she demanded, her outraged tones clearly reflecting her continued annoyance. 'They actually asked him to look up their wretched daughter when he came to England. So what does he do? Instead of staying with me as he'd planned, he rents this ancient pile, miles from anywhere, just so he can keep an eye on this stupid female who seems to have got herself into all sorts of trouble over a piece of land——'

'Wait a minute,' Hilary interrupted forcefully. 'Wait just a minute. Are you telling me that Leo—Matt,' she corrected herself impatiently, 'came over here because these people in Port Headland asked him to?'

'Yes! Can you believe it?' Gwen exclaimed. 'I do think it's the most infernal cheek! Instead of having Matt to myself, when I haven't seen him for months and months, I have to share him with this wretched woman who can't get her act together! It's diabolical! That's what it is! Selfish!'

'Yes,' Hilary agreed faintly. Staring rather blindly at Gwen, she ran the whole conversation through her head again. I'm a project? she thought, aghast. A bloody project? Oh, the bastard. Clenching her hands tight to stop them shaking, and unable to remain seated, she shoved her chair back and got to her feet.

'Oh, hell,' Gwen murmured, 'have I put my foot in it? Look, I'm sorry if she's a friend of yours or something. Maybe I got it wrong——'

'Oh, no, I'm sure you didn't,' Hilary denied

flatly, her voice cold, her body in shock. 'You mentioned land. What land?'

'Oh, I'm sure it hasn't anything to do——'

'What land?' Hilary repeated with ominous quietness.

'The land in the village,' Gwen admitted unhappily. 'Matt's been trying to get planning perm——'

Slamming her hand on the table, cutting off the other girl in mid-sentence, she denied frantically, 'No!' But what if it was true? Still staring at Gwen, her thoughts in chaos, the knowledge that Leo's interest had been at her parents' instigation for the moment forgotten, she tried to work out what possible interest planning permission could have for Leo. It was Ryan who was trying to get permission—and yet Gwen had just said. . .and hadn't Leo run out of the shop after Ryan? Hadn't he shown a rather disquieting interest in all the details of the demolished cottage? Which could only mean one thing. Leo and Ryan were in it together.

A whole host of emotions warring for supremacy—confusion, hurt, anger—she continued to stare unseeingly at Leo's sister. 'Oh, the bastard!' she exclaimed brokenly. 'The bloody bastard.' Barely registering Gwen's horrified face, she turned and whirled out, crashing the back door against the wall so hard that the echoes seemed to follow her fleeing figure.

She ran as hard as she could across the muddy

field, across the rickety bridge, and finally col-
lapsed beyond the line of oaks where the stream
curved round to mark the boundary of the
colonel's property. Her lungs heaving, she fell
against a tree, then slowly slid down the trunk
to sit at its foot, her arms wrapped tight round
her updrawn knees in an effort to hold in the
pain and shock that was robbing her of coherent
thought. She was shaking so much that everything seemed blurred, merged together.

'Ah, no, no,' she whispered, 'please, not Leo.
Please, please don't let it be Leo.' Her head
resting on her knees, she tried to contain the
pain that was clenching her stomach muscles
into a tight knot. Her teeth gritted together to
stop herself screaming, she rocked backwards
and forwards like a child, oblivious to the drizzle
that had begun while she'd been in the kitchen
with Gwen as disjointed sentences jostled in her
brain for supremacy. Any reasonably proficient
man can make a woman feel special. He's not
worth your tears. In property, he'd said, but he
hadn't said what sort, had he? Talkies time, he'd
said, yet he'd been curiously evasive. Hair and
clothing saturated, she fought desperately to
keep control.

His name wasn't even Leo, but then, what
did his name matter? He'd lied about so much
else, and it was quite clear now why he'd
wanted to know so much about Ryan, where he
was, what he'd done; he'd wanted to know how
much or how little Ryan had told her so that he

didn't make the same mistakes. It also became clear why he'd wanted to make love to her; to make her believe he cared, because if she cared for him who better to persuade the colonel to tell his friends on the council to let the plans go through? But if that was the case where did her parents come into it? And, if they had asked him to come, where did Ryan fit into it? Yet if he'd known Ryan first. . .and Mr Green had said Ryan had a partner, hadn't he? Then why had he told Gwen he knew her parents?

Coincidence? No, that was asking too much of credibility. So why? Pummelling her fists against her forehead, she tried to think. If he'd already known Ryan, which it now seemed he did, had he then looked up her parents deliberately? To find out what they knew? To see if she was there? Yes, that made more sense. Ryan must have assumed that she'd gone to stay with her parents when he left her. Yet why did Ryan have an Australian partner?

The thoughts jumbling and whirling in her head, she came to the conclusion that the details didn't really matter. All that mattered was that she had been the fool. Twice in one year. Two men so different in appearance and manner, yet both prepared to sacrifice her feelings on the altar of their ambition. Yet it was Leo's betrayal that so twisted the knife inside her. How could she have been so gullible? Had she learned nothing? As her tears continued to fall unheeded to mingle with the rain, her mouth twisted bitterly. The signs had all been there if only she'd had the gumption to read them.

Thinking back over the past year, a wasted year, a year out of her life, she found it quite incomprehensible now to understand how she had allowed a no-good rat like Ryan to almost destroy her. And not only that, she had compounded her stupidity by allowing herself to be duped by Leo. She had once embraced the world with her enthusiasm, laughed at life, had been filled with compassion for those less fortunate, and what was she now? An empty shell. A shadow of Hilary. Her family would be appalled at her cowardice. Don't let Ryan destroy you, Leo had said, and now it was equally true of himself. Being gullible was bad enough, but a coward to boot? Oh, no, she resolved, not twice; she wasn't going to waste another year of her life!

She found a damp tissue in her pocket and blew her nose hard, then, taking a long shaky breath and resolutely straightening her shoulders, she got stiffly to her feet. 'I'll not be a two-time loser, you bastard!'

CHAPTER FIVE

STARING round at the dark grey clouds scudding across the sky, at the almost violet light on the horizon, Hilary tilted her face and allowed the rain to sluice her tears away. The tree-tops were bowing in the rising wind, and it sounded as though they, too, were sighing. Moving back to the bridge, she halted for a moment to stare down at the sluggish water, and the wavering reflection thrown back at her made her feel like weeping forever. As she clenched her hands on the rail until they hurt, she fought to hate him, to make herself angry, not to give in to the terrible despair that kept threatening to overwhelm her. Her hair was like dripping rats' tails, her jeans and sweat-shirt plastered to her body, and she thought she wanted to die. And if I do, she vowed silently, I'll come back and bloody haunt you.

Wrapping her arms round herself in a futile attempt to retain some body-heat, she began the long walk back to the cottage. She didn't hear the car coming up the lane behind her, barely even registered it as it passed; it was only when a car door was violently slammed that she looked up, and froze. Staring at a very grim-looking Leo, she decided she wasn't ready for a confrontation so soon. Her resolution wavering, she stared round her in helpless panic.

'Where the hell have you been?' he demanded.

Dying inside, she wanted to cry, and if his words did nothing else they did at least stiffen her disintegrating spine. When he reached out to touch her, all the anger and disillusion exploded. 'Don't touch me!' she yelled, and like a little wet and muddy wildcat she wrenched herself free of his grip. 'Don't ever touch me again!' Drawing back her arm, she hit him as hard as she could across the face. 'You unscrupulous, lying bastard! Don't know Port Headland, don't know Ryan——'

'Hilary!' he roared. Pinning her arms to her sides, he was then forced to yank her hard against his body to protect his shins from her lashing feet. 'Calm down——'

'Calm down? Calm down? Why the hell should I?' she spat breathlessly. 'You wander into my life with your lies and arrogance, tell me to pull myself together, and then proceed to stab me in the back!'

'I have not stabbed you in the back, dammit! And keep still,' he thundered as Hilary wriggled futilely. In desperation he lifted her bodily off the ground so that she was helplessly pinned against his solid frame, and she discovered to her horror that hating him didn't in any way negate the way he could make her feel. As the familiar weakness spiralled through her she renewed her desperate struggles to be free.

'And I thought Ryan was a rat,' she gasped raggedly. 'You didn't even have the decency to use your own name, did you?'

'Hilary,' he broke in gently, 'you're soaking wet, cold, upset, and this is neither the time nor the place, but there was a reason——'

'Oh, yes, an excellent reason,' she retorted bitterly. 'If I'd known your real name I might have found out that you were Ryan's partner, mightn't I? And that would never have done! Stupid, gullible Hilary. It was almost too easy, wasn't it?'

'Hilary——'

'Don't "Hilary" me! Don't ever "Hilary" me!' she shouted. 'Your little game is over. A project!' she spat. 'A blasted project! Had to sort her out, did you? A silly little girl who'd got herself into trouble! And then the silly little girl went and believed the glib tales she was told by the great Australian male, didn't she? Well? Nothing to say? No excuses?' she sobbed.

His face curiously bleak, he slowly released her. 'I know Port Headland, yes. I know your parents, and your brother and his wife,' he said quietly, his voice totally without inflexion. 'I stayed with them. They talked about you, of course they did, but not once were the words "silly little girl" mentioned. Ever. Your family were worried about you. I was coming to England——'

'And oh, what a coincidence that it was to the same part of the country!' she butted in sarcastically.

'Yes. It *was* a coincidence. They do happen, you know. I said I would be happy to look you up, which I was. Why not? I'd seen pictures of you. . .a home movie; you were a beautiful young woman—why shouldn't I agree to look you up? It's not a crime.'

'No, it's not a crime,' she agreed with a bitter little laugh. 'So why deny it?'

'Because you'd have put even more barriers up,' he explained wearily. 'Wouldn't you? If I'd said your parents had asked me to come, do you think I'd have got you to tell me about Ryan?'

'But there was no need, was there? You knew all about him.'

'Did I? How did I know all about him?'

'I don't know, do I?' she exclaimed, her voice breaking. 'I only know that you do! That you conspired with him to cheat me. How could you?' she yelled, her control slipping. 'Knowing what I'd been through? If you wanted planning permission for the land so badly, why couldn't you just ask?'

'Presumably because I'm devious and unscrupulous,' he said with such awful softness that she winced. 'You really believe all this garbage?' he asked incredulously. 'Well, do you?'

'Yes!' she hissed. Looking very much like the arrogant duchess he had once accused her of being, despite her wet and muddy state, she drew herself up to her full height, and stated with flat finality, 'You can both do as you please regarding the land. I no longer care. I have no intention of wasting any more of my life. Neither of you are worth it.'

When he only continued to stare at her, his eyes narrowed, almost black, Hilary felt a moment of panic. The rain had darkened his brown hair, and rivulets of water dripped down a face that looked to be carved from teak. The gentleness had gone from his expression and Hilary took an involuntary step back. 'You've won, Leo,' she managed quietly, 'and I hope with all my heart that you find it a pyrrhic victory.'

Retaining his grim silence, he continued to watch her. There was only the sound of the strengthening wind that stirred her wet curls and plastered the sweat-shirt tighter against her shivering frame. A small defiant kitten against a Great Dane and about as effective, she thought tiredly. Unable to bear any more, she swung away to stumble over the ploughed field. She no longer even cared if it was the direction she wanted to go. Her burst of temper had left her empty, drained of feeling, and all she wanted now was to crawl away somewhere to lick her wounds in private.

He hadn't denied it, had he? If he *had* denied it there could have been some hope. Only he hadn't.

When she finally reached the cottage it was just getting dark. Slumping at the kitchen table, she stared blankly ahead of her. She ought to get out of her wet clothes, have a hot bath, make herself a hot drink, only that seemed to require too much effort. She felt chilled right through—not just her body, but her heart and mind. Too tired and cold to think any more, she put her head down on her arms on the table and, without any idea that she was about to do so, she burst into tears. Long shuddering sobs shook her slight frame as she poured out her hurt and misery. She cried until she could cry no more, until she felt sick, until her head ached, and when she finally stumbled up to bed she merely threw off her clothes and climbed, shivering, between the icy covers.

There was no warm sun to greet Hilary next morning when she awoke. No blue skies, just the same depressing grey she had grown used to, and as the events of yesterday flooded relentlessly into her mind her eyes filled with helpless tears. Ever since she had come to Norfolk the skies had been grey, and she suddenly longed for warmth. For hot sun to drive away the chill inside her. Kind skies and balmy breezes instead of the cutting east wind off the marshes. It would be the end of summer in Australia, and people would be longing for the winter. Tired of brown grass and dried riverbeds, of the brown dusty landscape, they would examine blue, blue skies for the sight of a cloud.

Rolling on to her back, she stared unhappily at too many clouds that raced each other across the low sky. Twenty-four hours since she had last looked out on that scene, watched the same blue curtains stir in the draught through the ill-fitting window-frame.

'Oh, Leo, why?' she asked helplessly. Sniffing and wiping away her tears with her fists like a child, she climbed out and hastily dragged on her dressing-gown. As she pushed her cold hands into the pockets, her fingers encountered the stiff crackle of paper and her resolve not to give in nearly broke. Leo's note. Taking it out, she ripped it into tiny pieces then tossed the fragments into the bucket that still stood on the dresser like some awful avant-garde ornament.

Shivering uncontrollably, she went downstairs. Unable to face the thought of food, she made herself some tea. She'd like to run away, not have to see him again, but there was no one she could go to stay with. She couldn't afford to stay in a boarding-house, no matter how cheap it might be, so she'd have to stay in the cottage. Yet the thought of being cooped up within four walls all day and every day until Leo went back to Australia was unthinkable. She'd go mad.

She could go back to work, she supposed, only if she did that everyone would want to know why. Nobody in their right mind gave up their holiday in favour of work! Well then, she would explore Norfolk, she decided defiantly. It was only for another week. Seven days. That wasn't so long, was it? If she left early each morning and came home late at night there was very little likelihood of her meeting Leo. Although it was hardly likely he would want to seek her out.

If he had looked ashamed it might have been easier to bear. Only he hadn't, just quietly angry, and bitter, she thought with a frown. Why the hell should he look bitter? Deciding that it must be because his plans had been thwarted, she firmly dismissed him from her thoughts.

After she had washed and dressed in warm cord trousers, leather boots and a thick sweater, she this time took the precaution of collecting her anorak before going out to her car and driving off in the direction of Great Yarmouth.

When you had lots of things to do, goals to achieve, time flew past. When you had nothing to do but kill time, it dragged incredibly slowly. She had intended to return to the cottage in late evening, eleven at the least, but by seven o'clock she was so thoroughly depressed that she drove home. Most of Norfolk seemed to consist of holiday towns, geared for tourists, and the tourist season didn't start until late May. In early April it was lonely, cold, wet and empty.

Unclocking her front door, she tossed her anorak on to the wall-peg. She slammed the door and leaned back against for a moment. She felt exhausted and so very cold. Her eyes bleak, she surveyed her small domain that, instead of the retreat it had once represented, was now a prison. She trailed unhappily into the kitchen, picked up the kettle then thumped it down again. She was sick of tea. Wandering out again like an unhappy ghost, she went into her workroom, turned on the light and stared at the bench. The tools, pieces of wood, looked abandoned, dead, and with an impatient sigh she snapped the light off again. She closed the door and dragged herself wearily up the stairs; as she pushed open her bedroom door she screamed in fright when a dark figure materialised out of the gloom.

'For God's sake!' Leo exclaimed. Catching her arm, he dragged her into the room. 'It's only me!'

'And that's supposed to make me feel better?' she asked bitterly. 'And let go my damned arm!' Shrugging herself free, she snapped on the light. 'What are you doing in my bedroom?'

'Looking for you! What else would I be doing?'

'How the hell should I know? Get out!'

'No. I want to talk to you! I had hoped,' he continued with the same bitterness she was using, 'that you might have calmed down by now.'

'Calmed down?' she screamed. 'Why the hell should I calm down?' Despairing and anguished, she lashed out at him and he caught her arm in a punishing grip.

'It would have been more to the point if you'd attacked Ryan,' he said brutally, 'because, despite your lousy opinion of me, I've done nothing to deliberately hurt you. Neither have I done anything of which I need be ashamed!'

'Then you have a lousy code of ethics!' she snapped. Pushing roughly past him, she went to stand at the window, her back to him.

'No, Hilary, I do not,' he told her grimly. 'Now, whether you like it or not, we are going to talk.'

'We have nothing to talk about!'

'Yes we do! Like, for instance, how I'm supposed to have known Ryan.'

'Supposed?' she sneered.

'Yes, supposed!' he ground out. Striding over to her, he caught her arm and swung her round to face him.

'Don't touch me!' she yelled instinctively.

'Why? Afraid you'll respond?' he asked nastily.

'No, I'm damned well not!' she denied furiously, her eyes wide and startled as they clashed with his. 'You leave me quite cold.'

'I didn't yesterday!'

'Yesterday was yesterday, and, as you so rightly pointed out, any reasonably proficient man can make a woman feel special. Well, let me tell you that any reasonably proficient woman can fool a man into thinking—ow!' she yelled as he grasped her shoulders in a painful grip.

'Meaning?' he asked, oh, so softly, a warning glitter in his eyes.

A warning Hilary chose to ignore. Why the hell should he have it all his own way? Did he think he was the only one who could lie and cheat? Facing him defiantly, her mouth a thin, bitter line, she articulated, 'Meaning it wasn't you I was responding to.' She thought for a moment that he was going to hit her and she leaned hastily back. Only he didn't, merely narrowed his eyes further, then pulled her against him so tight that she could feel every sinew and muscle from knee to chest, and a lick of frightened excitement curled along her nerves.

'Then pretend this is Ryan,' he grated savagely. Before she could stop him, his mouth was against hers, parting her mouth in a travesty of a kiss that forced her lips against her teeth.

Frightened and helpless, she made incoherent little sounds of distress in her throat as her hands desperately tried to push him away.

Then, suddenly, she was free as Leo thrust her away with enough force to slam her back against the window and set it rattling behind her. 'Now you listen to me,' he bit out furiously. 'I met your parents by accident. I crashed my plane in their back yard. Mike dragged me clear and carried me into the house. When I regained consciousness it was to find that I'd injured my spine and the doctor had ordered that I was to stay put, otherwise there was the possibility that I'd end up a cripple. Are you actually listening to me?' he demanded harshly.

'Yes,' she muttered as she deliberately refused to even consider the implications of his statement, of that strong body being in a wheelchair, diminished, the arrogance dimmed.

'I'm not a particularly patient man, and the thought of lying flat on my back for weeks made me feel almost suicidal, and if it hadn't been for your parents—well, suffice to say that they were marvellous——'

'Well, they would be, wouldn't they?' she interrupted sarcastically, 'seeing as they were just about to send you on a spying mission!'

'Shut up!' he gritted. When she subsided, her face mutinous, he continued grimly, 'Lying on my back in their spare room, bored and in pain, forced to lie still, I watched the television that your parents were kind enough to install. I listened to the radio, tapes, watched videos, and found no interest in anything. In desperation your mother gave me some home movies they'd made over the years, and I watched a chubby five-year-old with a cheeky grin and eyes like pansies. I watched her grow into a tomboy with a smile that encompassed the world; eyes with the devil inside. I watched her laugh. I watched her cry and I watched her grow into a beautiful assured young woman with the same infectious grin. A woman who loved life, people. A woman who would tackle the hardest tasks for those she loved, who met life head-on and never cried craven. And I wanted her! For me!'

Despite the fact that she wanted to weep, and she was shaking so badly inside that it was a wonder she could still stand up straight at all, she snorted derisively, because she was too afraid to believe his words. Forcing herself to meet his gaze, she asked sarcastically, 'Finished?'

'No, Hilary, I have not finished, and you are going to stand there and listen until I have. I did not have to be persuaded to come and see you. No one twisted my arm. I hadn't been planning to come to England, but I wanted to meet you. Gwen was just an excuse, and she lived in Norfolk. When I found out what was going on I persuaded the colonel to go for a little holiday— and then,' he continued angrily when Hilary snorted derisively again, 'when I did meet you, I couldn't believe my eyes. You looked nothing like the girl in the movies.'

'And so, just like Don Quixote, you determined to put my windmill straight! Very laudable, Leo, but hardly believable. Well, go on, don't stop there, I'm sure the rest is just as fascinating—presumably that, yes, you knew Ryan, but when you flew over to find out why the hell he couldn't get something so simple as planning permission you decided to do something about it yourself, and there was guillible little Hilary, all ready and waiting to fall into your arms. Get round Hilary, and, hey presto, you'd get your plans passed!'

'Don't be so damned ridiculous!'

'It is not ridiculous!' she screamed. 'It all fits!'

'Yes, it fits,' he said quietly, his eyes like stone, flat and empty. 'So does my interpretation. I asked you to trust me, Hilary. Trust. A small word that can mean the difference between happiness and despair. You are obviously determined to believe that I deliberately and maliciously set out to destroy you, knowing as I did how much you had already been hurt.'

'Why not? It's only what I've come to expect from men, isn't it?' she asked bitterly. Too far along her own road to hell to draw back now, she continued rashly, her eyes wide in feigned surprise. 'Or don't tell me that all those questions about Ryan were simply so that you could track him down and make him pay the money back?'

After a little tense silence that made it seem as though the very air were holding it breath, he said very evenly, and with dangerous softness. 'Yes.' Taking a folded piece of paper from his pocket, he handed it to her. 'It would seem that I fell in love with an illusion. I thought you had courage, guts, that you were someone bright and exciting; but one set-back and you crumble, don't you, Hilary? Blame everyone but yourself. Well, so be it. I've had enough. But let me just tell you this; self-pity will destroy you far more

assuredly then Ryan could ever have done.'
With a last disparaging look at her, he turned
and walked out.

Shocked and disbelieving, she slowly opened
the piece of paper with hands that shook uncontrollably, and it took her a moment to realise
what it was. A cheque for the exact amount of
money she had given Ryan.

'Oh, dear God,' she whispered.

Slumping down on the side of the bed, she
stared blankly at the cheque in her hand. He
hadn't been lying. He'd been telling the truth.
And she'd accused. . . Yet it wasn't entirely her
fault, was it? If he'd explained at the beginning—and it didn't cancel out the fact that he'd
lied to her, did it? Spied on her. Didn't alter the
fact that he'd deliberately sought her out
because of her parents. And the lovemaking?
What category did that come under? And how
on earth had he got the money out of Ryan
anyway? Ryan wouldn't have given it up willingly, she knew.

As she rubbed her hand tiredly across her
forehead she stared at the cheque until the
writing blurred and danced before her eyes, and
every word she had flung at him, every insult,
seemed burned indelibly into her brain. Desperately needing to justify her own actions, minim-
ise her behaviour, she thought it all through
again from the beginning until it made even less
sense than it had before.

With a long shivery sigh, knowing she had no

choice, not if she ever wanted to make things right, she climbed wearily to her feet. Dear God, but he'd been angry. She walked across to the dresser flattened the cheque out and laid it beside the bucket. Going downstairs, not bothering to collect her coat, she went out and pulled the back door to behind her. As a final act of perversity, the moon chose that moment to sail majestically behind the clouds, leaving Hilary to grope her way along the lane in the pitch dark.

Taking a deep breath and straightening her slumping shoulders, she pushed open the back door of the colonel's house, and as she saw the dim light from the lounge spilling out into the hall she walked in that direction.

Leo was standing at the drinks cabinet in the corner, his back to her, yet it didn't prevent his knowing instantly who it was.

'Go away, Hilary,' he said wearily.

'I came to apologise for hitting you,' she began determinedly, 'and to thank you for the cheque.'

'Fine. You've thanked me. Goodbye,' he concluded flatly. Sloshing more whisky into his already half-full glass, he walked across to the armchair and sprawled untidily.

A mutinous glint in her lovely eyes, she glared at him. 'If you hadn' t lied to me——'

'Oh, for God's sake!' he exploded. 'What was I supposed to do? Come knocking on your door to say your mother was worried about you? Would you please write and tell her what the hell was going on?'

'Well, it would have been more honest,' she muttered.

'Oh, honest, is it? Was it honest to lie to your family? Hurt them? Was it honest to play the damned tragedy queen, driving everyone insane with your self-pity?'

'It wasn't self-pity!'

'What was it, then?' he asked angrily.

'I was hurt, dammit!'

'So are a lot of people! It's a fact of life! You're twenty-seven, for God's sake, not seven! Life's full of knocks. It's not a damned fairy-story.'

'I never said it was!' she snapped. Furious, and hurt, and quite forgetting she was supposed to be being conciliatory, she demanded, 'What was I supposed to do? Just shrug it off? Pretend it never happened? Is it so wrong to want a bit of sympathy?'

'Sympathy?' he queried in astonishment. 'You didn't want sympathy! You wanted acclamation!'

Disbelief momentarily robbed her of words; then she exploded, 'You rotten, self-centred toad! I didn't ask you to come and pry into my life——'

'No,' he interrupted, 'your mother did! And why? Because her precious daughter was too selfish, too bound up in her own misery to care that other people were hurt! How the hell do you think they felt when their darling Hilary was too busy to go out for her brother's wedding?'

'But I explained——'

'Explained?' he cut in ruthlessly as he struggled to his feet. Striding across the room, he thrust his harsh, angry face towards hers, 'Oh, yes, Hilary, you explained, and in such a way that they thought you couldn't be bothered.'

'No!'

'Yes!' he hissed. 'Too wrapped up in your precious Ryan to bother!'

'No! How could I tell them?' she asked, her voice anguished. 'How could I explain that I didn't have the money to go? That the man they had warned me against had taken it. . .'

'How could you not? Do you think they wouldn't rather have known the truth than believe you'd grown too selfish to care?'

'But it wasn't true,' she whispered helplessly.

'No, but they didn't know that, did they?' he asked more moderately.

Her eyes fixed widely on his, despair and unhappiness in their depths, she asked miserably, 'You said you wanted me; how could you do that if you thought I was selfish and self-centred?'

'Oh, grow up,' he said in disgust. 'Even believing the worst, you can still want someone. You can't turn feelings off just because your mind tells you they're rubbish!'

'And is that what I am? Rubbish?' she asked quietly, her voice husky and broken.

'No,' he denied wearily as he turned away. 'Go home, Hilary.'

'And the lovemaking?' she perservered, desperately needing to know.

Turning only his head, his eyes more black than she had ever seen them, he asked flatly, 'What do you think?'

'I don't know,' she admitted. And she didn't, couldn't at that moment conceive of any reason, however remote, why he would want to make love to her.

'Then I suggest you go away and think about it.' Turning his back in dismissal, he stared down into the fire.

With one last look at him, she turned and trailed out. More hurt, bewildered and confused than she would ever have believed possible such a short time ago, she walked into the dark cottage and up to bed.

CHAPTER SIX

MENTAL and physical exhaustion ensured that Hilary slept deeply, and it was well after ten when she finally stirred. Stiff and cold, she stared bleakly before her as the events of yesterday rushed into her mind. Think about it, Leo had said. About what? Impatiently thrusting the covers aside, she hurried into the bathroom. Finding that the water was scalding hot, since she'd left the immersion heater on all night, she had a bath. She didn't now even have to worry about the size of the electricity bill, nor any other bills, come to that. The knowledge didn't make her feel any better.

All that day she thought about his words, considered them, agonised over them, tried to justify her behaviour that now seemed to bear no justification at all. If he had loved her, or begun to love her, which she still found utterly unbelievable, her accusations would have successfully killed it. Wouldn't they? Yet it wasn't entirely her fault. Hadn't he been guilty too? Or had she become so warped that everyone's motives became suspect? Unable to settle, she trailed round the small cottage, picking things up, putting them down again, with no clear idea of what to do. Yet she didn't want him to go

back to Australia thinking so badly of her. She
wanted to make everything all right. But how?
Halting in front of the mirror in the front room,
the mirror that he had forced her to stare into,
she winced. She looked terrible. Her eyes were
dull, with dark shadows beneath them, her face
white, ghost-like, her hair lifeless. God, what a
mess. She looked about fifty, haggard and ill.
And if she went to see him now it was very
likely that her appearance would rekindle his
feelings, wasn't it? He was probably even now
thanking his lucky stars for a narrow escape.
She wasn't even sure how she felt about him.
Not for definite. She'd liked him, enjoyed his
lovemaking, but how much of her feelings were
generated by rebound? Had she only responded
because she'd needed to be loved?

Oh, Mum, what a mess your daughter has got
herself into, and all because of her silly pride,
her determination to lash out first before anyone
could lash back! And had her mother really
thought she had become so selfish? And Mike?
And her brother? Staring listlessly at herself,
Hilary suddenly felt such an overwhelming
longing to hear their voices again, make it right,
that, without stopping to consider it further, she
ran quickly upstairs to get her purse. She was
halfway, out of the cottage door before she
remembered the time-difference between
England and Australia. They were about ten
hours in front and if she rang them now it
would be the middle of the night. Her shoulders

slumping, she turned to go back in. Yet the thought of being cooped up indoors for another few hours made her feel almost suicidal. With a long sigh, she turned and pulled the door shut. She'd go for a walk—maybe some fresh air would clarify her thoughts.

Whether consciously or unconsciously, she found herself beside the ground where the cottage she had bought with Ryan had once stood. Such an uninspiring vista to bring so much heartache, and she found now that the sight of it no longer had the power to hurt her. There was a 'Sold' sticker on the board, and she stood gazing at it for a moment as though it might provide a magic solution to all her problems.

'Marvellous news, isn't it?' Frank Green said from behind her.

Startled, she swung round and gave him a lame smile. 'Yes,' she admitted with no clear idea whether it was or wasn't.

'Pity we didn't think of it ourselves,' he continued wryly. 'No doubt took Leo all of five minutes to think up that scheme! And I call myself a businessman! Oh, well, best get back to the shop else I'll have a queue of old women all clacking at me.' With a beaming smile and an avuncular pat on the arm, he added, 'I'm real glad for you, lass. So'll the colonel be.' He gave a little wave and walked briskly off towards his shop.

What hadn't they thought of themselves? she wondered with a frown. What scheme? They'd only sold the land, hadn't they? Staring blankly at the rubble, all that remained of the cottage, she tried to remember the exact words Leo had used when he'd given her the cheque. Or *she* had used. She had sarcastically asked him if he'd tracked Ryan down in order to make him pay it back, and he'd said yes. Was that the scheme Mr Green had meant?

Perching on the remains of a brick wall, she tried to go back over everything that had happened since Leo had arrived. His behaviour, the things he'd said, trying with her new knowledge of him to find flaws in his reasoning, and then wondered drearily why she bothered. She knew in her heart that he had told the truth, and it had been herself at fault for so lacking trust in his integrity. Levering herself tiredly to her feet, she walked despondently back to the cottage. There was no need to stay in England now, was there? Thanks to Leo she could afford to go out to Australia. Standing thoughtfully in the tiny kitchen, she suddenly turned and went out again. She would ring the agency, give in her notice, and as soon as she was free she would go out to her parents. She didn't want to stay here—not without Leo, she finally admitted. As she came to a halt in front of the phone-box Hilary faced her feelings squarely. She was in love with him. Not like with Ryan, a sort of frantic grasping at straws, in love with the idea of love, romance. This was different, a need deep inside, a feeling of being only half a person without him. And, if she went to Australia, mightn't there be a chance—however remote— that they would meet? Pulling open the heavy door, she lifted the receiver and dialled the number of her office, then spoke quickly and earnestly with her boss.

As she replaced the receiver with a sad little gesture she felt her eyes fill with tears. She hadn't deserved their kindness, their good wishes—she'd hardly been a boon companion of late. She didn't even need to work out her notice, just go in any time she felt like it to collect any personal belongings. She felt dreadfully guilty letting them down about the Rome and Athens trip, but even that they smoothed over, told her not to worry. Closing the door of the telephone-box, she walked slowly back to the cottage. All that remained now was to fill in the time until she could ring her mother.

At ten o'clock that evening, she walked back along the lane. Placing a pile of coins on the box in front of her, she slowly dialled the number.

They did more crying than actual talking, half-formed sentences, apologies, abandoned almost before they were begun. Then she had to say hello to Mike, then her mother again, with more laughter and tears and a promise that she would go out. Yes, very soon. She would ring next week. Yes, she had the fare, she would explain everything when they met. No, she no longer saw Ryan. Neither of them mentioned Leo.

Her arms hugged around herself, she stood in

the phone-box for a long time after she'd replaced the receiver and it seemed quite incomprehensible to her now that she hadn't contacted her mother before. It had all been so incredibly easy.

Walking slowly home, her hands pushed into her jacket pockets, Hilary smiled to herself. Soon she would see them, but first thing in the morning, before she booked her flight, packed up her belongings, she must see Leo, try and make him understand. Ask his forgiveness.

She lay awake for a long time that night, going over the conversation with her mother, trying to work out what she should say to Leo, and she rehearsed so many and varied conversations that she thought she'd go mad. What did you say to a man who thought you were rubbish? How could you refute it when just the memory of his scathing comments made your eyes fill with tears?

When she woke in the morning, she pulled on her dressing-gown and went down to the kitchen to make some tea. Ryan was lounging at the kitchen table, and she halted in shock.

'Hello, Hilary,' he greeted mildly.

The smile he gave her was familiar, full of charm, and yet she was now able to see it for what it was; totally false and lacking in warmth. Smiles came from within, they weren't just a facial movement, and she stared at him assessingly as she wondered how she could have been such a fool.

'Go away, Ryan,' she said flatly. Turning away from him, she filled the kettle and set it on the stove.

As he leaned his elbows on the table he observed maliciously, 'You look terrible.'

Refusing to be drawn into a discussion, she retorted bluntly, 'Just say what you have to say and go.'

'Very well. I came to say I was sorry. Belated, I know, but that was why I came, and to make sure you got the cheque.'

'Sorry?' she queried in disbelief. 'You really expect me to believe that? As though you were some kind, caring person, who had never caused me a moment's upset? And you really expect me to believe that the return of the cheque was your idea? Come on, Ryan, gullible I might once have been. Stupid I am not.'

'No? Oh, well, please yourself,' he retorted indifferently, then, with a rather nasty gleam in his blue eyes, he murmured, 'Flying a bit high, aren't you? Or do you like falling flat on your face?'

'Meaning?' she asked icily.

'Verlander, my dear Hilary. Verlander.'

'Who?' she asked blankly.

'Oh, come on, don't play me for a fool! Matt Verlander—tycoon playboy of the outback!'

'Leo?' she exclaimed.

'Leo? Who the hell's Leo?'

Suddenly remembering a similarly pointless conversation with Gwen, she snapped, 'Matt is

Leo! I meant that I didn't know his name was
Verlander.'

'Oh.' Still staring at her rather speculatively,
he suddenly burst out laughing. 'You don't
know who he is, do you?'

'Judging by your expression, no; neither do I
want you to enlighten me!' she said hastily.
She'd already got herself into all sorts of trouble
listening to other people's opinions, and she
wasn't going to make that mistake again. 'And
if you've come to try and make trouble, Ryan,
don't bother.'

'Mm, deserved that, didn't I?' he queried
almost gently, and Hilary stared at him in astonishment. 'But I am sorry,' he insisted.

He looked so contrite that for a moment she
was in danger of actually believing him, until
common sense came to her aid. With a derisive
snort, she turned away to make the tea. 'The
day you ever feel contrition for your actions is
the day the sea freezes over,' she said
scathingly.

'We had something good once. . .'

'I thought we had something good,' she corrected quietly. 'Only then someone destroyed
my confidence, my ability to trust, and, looking
at you now, I can't for the life of me see how I
could possibly have thought myself in love with
someone so shallow, so completely self-
centred.' And it was true. She'd once worried
that when she saw him again the old feelings
might come back, but she felt nothing. Leaning

on the back of the chair, she asked casually, 'Why did you write and tell me you'd never loved me? That was pretty malicious, wasn't it? Even for you.'

'Because I wanted you to hate me,' he explained simply. 'I thought it would be easier for you if you hated me.'

'Oh, I did that,' she told him flatly, 'but if that was your intention which I doubt, don't you think it might have been kinder to have left me with a few illusions?'

'Maybe. I never meant to hurt you, you know.'

Giving him a look of disgust, she turned away to get a cup and saucer out of the cupboard. 'Go away, Ryan; we have nothing further to say to each other.'

'All right,' he agreed.

Surprised at such easy acquiescence, she stared at him suspiciously.

'Just tell me where Verlander is,' he concluded as he got to his feet and came to stand beside her.

'Why?'

'Because, my dear Hilary, he owes me some money.'

'Owes you some. . .' As all the old, nasty suspicions rose again, she hastily squashed them. 'Why does he owe you money?' she asked. This time she was determined to get it in black and white. Ask, not assume.

His expression blank, he stared at her for long moments. 'Did you or did you not get a cheque?'

'Yes.'

'Then that is the money he owes me.'

'Ah,' she exclaimed softly. 'You paid Leo, Leo paid me. . .'

'Don't be bloody stupid!' he exclaimed pityingly. 'Verlander bought the land from me at a grossly undervalued price! He then sold it. . .'

'At a vastly inflated price?' she guessed, her face suddenly alight with laughter. Now how had Leo managed that? Enjoying the irony of it, and actually quite pleased to discover that Ryan hadn't turned over a new leaf after all, she continued smoothly, 'And might I remind you, Ryan, that it was my money in the first place, not yours? Now go away—and if you are thinking of offering Leo violence, I should forget it; he'd make mincemeat of you.'

'Just tell me where he is.'

'I don't know, and even if I did I wouldn't tell you.' Ignoring him, she looked down to put milk and sugar into her cup.

'OK,' he agreed with another little shrug. 'I expect someone in the village will tell——'

When he broke off in the middle of the sentence, she glanced up at him curiously and was completely taken by surprise when he pulled her into his arms and kissed her. With a cross little grunt, she shoved him away. 'That wasn't very amusing, Ryan,' she bit out as she wiped the back of her hand across her mouth.

'Not to be compared with the tycoon, eh?' eh asked nastily. 'Well, I shouldn't pin your hopes to that particular mast, sweetheart,' he sneered. 'He's no more likely to marry you than I was.' With a taunting smile, he opened the back door and sauntered out.

Slamming it after him, a look of disgust on her face, Hilary poured out her tea then carried the cup to the table and sat nursing it in her palms. Who'd said anything about marriage? Thoughts of that had never even entered her head. Had they? But a tycoon? How much of that little statement was truth she wondered, and how much Ryan's exaggeration? He didn't look like a tycoon. Playboy, yes, she admitted reluctantly; she could well imagine him wining and dining beautiful Australian socialites. But a tycoon?

The tea forgotten, she gazed blankly through the window. Think about it, Leo had instructed her when she'd asked about the lovemaking. Only she didn't need to think about it, not really, not about the lovemaking itself at any rate—it was indelibly printed on her mind in glorious Technicolor. Her expression arrested, she wondered if that was what he'd meant. That she'd no need to query it because it had been so special.

'Verlander,' she whispered to herself. 'Matt Verlander.' Remembering the cheque, she went upstairs to get it, she flattened it out and stared at the signature. M. H. Verlander. 'H'? she wondered. What did the 'H' stand for? Harry? Horace? Hippocrates?

With a little smile, she smoothed her hand across the creased piece of paper. She'd automatically assumed that it was from Ryan, only of course it wasn't, and if she had been thinking rationally before she would have known it couldn't possibly have been from him. No way would he ever part with his money willingly— then she grinned to herself, because that was precisely what he had done. Only how had Leo managed to persuade him? Ryan must have known the market value of the land. . . It also meant that Leo had gone to an awful lot of trouble on her behalf. Why? It couldn't really be because of a home movie, could it? Don't speculate, she warned herself. If you want to know, go and ask. Right. Only this time she would not lose her temper, she promised herself. They would talk properly, rationally.

With a sort of sick excitement inside, she washed, and dressed in a soft blue wool dress that just reached her boot tops. Brushing out her hair and applying some make-up, something she hadn't done for ages, she put on her mac. She placed the cheque in her bag, let herself out through the back way and, checking that Ryan had gone, because she didn't want him following her, she walked along the lane, careful not to trip on muddy ruts.

It seemed to take an enormous amount of courage to actually walk up to the door and knock. Getting no reply, she hesitantly pushed open the back door. Leo was standing at the

Aga wielding the frying-pan with what appeared to be a great deal of skill, and the smell of frying bacon made Hilary's mouth water. He was dressed in close-fitting grey trousers that emphasised the length of his legs and a short-sleeved cotton-knit shirt, also in grey, a striped butcher's apron protecting them from fat splashes. His face was absorbed, and Hilary stood quietly, studying him for a few moments. How could she not have known she was in love with him? she wondered—it seemed impossible to believe that she had looked at him, touched him, made love with him, and not known until yesterday. She had known she liked him, enjoyed his company, his humour, gentleness, so why had she never admitted that she loved? Just the sight of him made her go weak, ache, and the thought of never seeing him again, never being able to touch him, was a twisting pain in her heart. Only what good did it do to admit it? He certainly didn't look as though he felt the same. He looked remote, distant, and very, very unapproachable. Like a tycoon. He didn't look the sort of man to forgive and forget either.

The soft little click the door made when she closed it caused him to turn his head, and not by one flicker of an eyelash did he betray any emotion of her entrance. He merely looked her up and down from her booted feet to her wind-blown hair, then returned his attention to the stove, and Hilary almost turned and went out again.

Almost. Hovering uncertainly, she jumped when he barked impatiently, 'Either come in or go out. There's coffee in the pot if you want it,' he added more mildly.

'Thank you,' she whispered. Placing her bag on the table, she halted beside him as she looked vaguely round for a mug.

'Cups in the cupboard above your head,' he said brusquely.

Reaching for a cup, her arm accidentally brushed his and she flinched as though she'd been burned, which brought forth another acid comment.

'I don't bloody bite!'

'No,' she agreed helplessly, not in the least convinced. She quickly took down a cup and reached out to grasp the handle of the coffee pot, only to have her wrist gripped in punishing fingers.

'For God's sake, Hilary, the thing's red hot! Use the cloth! Don't you have any sense?'

'Apparently not,' she whispered as her eyes filled with stinging tears. She wanted desperately to hold him, make things right, only she didn't have the courage. Pouring out the coffee with a shaking hand, adding milk and sugar, she went to sit at the table. She felt about as poised as a baby elephant taking his first steps, she thought miserably. Take on the world and never cry craven, he'd said. Fat chance.

'Do you want anything to eat?' he asked
abruptly.

'No, thank you.' Any appetite she might have
had was now completely gone.

With a little grunt, he returned to his cooking
and she regretted her abrupt refusal. Any conversation, even if it was only about food, was
better than this stalemate. Staring at his back,
she tried to conjure up the image of him lover-
like, tender, and failed. The scene she had
envisaged before she'd come of herself apologis-
ing nicely, and thanking him, of Leo smiling
gently, bore absolutely no relation to the reality.
He looked as though he'd never smiled in his
life.

'I'm sorry,' she apologised. Her voice
sounded over-loud in the silent kitchen, and she
wished she'd kept quiet.

'For what?'

'Being so rude, and——'

'Oh, not rude, Hilary,' he denigrated.
'Insulting.'

'Insulting, then,' she agreed quietly, determined not to lose her temper, although if he
was going to carry on in that vein the chances of
her keeping it for very long were absolutely nil.
Taking a deep breath, she continued, 'And I also
came to thank you. For explaining about my
family. I rang them,' she added lamely in the
face of his indifference. Lapsing into silence, she
sipped her now unwanted coffee and only
looked up when he came to sit opposite her, a

large plate of bacon and eggs before him. He appeared totally oblivious of her presence and didn't even look up as far as she was aware. Clearing her throat, she said hesitantly, 'Ryan came to see me.'

'I know, although I'm not altogether sure he would appreciate your effort to dress up. He probably preferred you in your dressing-gown—or not,' he added insultingly.

'I didn't dress up for him!' she exclaimed. 'Or undress, come to that—and what do you mean you know?'

Looking up, his face hard, he explained, 'I came to see you earlier. I thought that maybe I'd been a bit harsh last night.'

But now he didn't think he'd been harsh at all. Why? What had made him change his mind? The mere fact of Ryan's being in her cottage? Or. . .or something else. Her mouth twisting, she suddenly knew exactly what that something else was. Leo had seen Ryan kissing her, he must have done, and put his own interpretation on it. 'You saw Ryan kiss me, didn't you?'

'Did I?'

'Yes,' she agreed thoughtfully, 'and Ryan kissed me because he'd seen you.' Right to the end, he couldn't resist putting a spoke into someone else's wheel. Especially if the wheel happened to be hers. What a little rat. Putting her elbows on the table, she leaned forward and explained quietly, 'He saw you, that's why he kissed me.'

'So I would assume,' he agreed indifferently. He got to his feet, took his empty plate across to the sink and poured himself some coffee.

'But you still think he was there by my invitation? And that busy little brain of yours presumably also believes that I was in my dressing-gown because he stayed the night. Is that it?'

'What you do or do not do is no concern of mine——'

'No,' she interrupted, 'but you seem to be accusing me of exactly the same things I accused you of—or at least had to ask about. You aren't usually so lacking in confidence,' she couldn't resist taunting.

'Confidence?' he asked softly. His expression was bland, unreadable, but there was a definite glint in his eye that made her pulse begin to race.

'You once seemed to think that you were reasonably proficient; enough, anyway, to make me forget Ryan. You think Ryan is proficient enough to make me forget you?'

His eyes narrowed on her face, he put his cup down, stripped off his apron, and walked slowly to stand beside her chair so that she was forced to look up at him. 'And is he?' he asked softly.

Swallowing convulsively in an effort to dislodge the hard, dry lump in her throat, she shook her head.

'No,' he agreed. His whole body still, poised, his eyes still holding hers, he continued in the same soft voice. 'Go through into the lounge. It's more comfortable.'

For what? she wondered. She got stiffly to her feet and walked obediently through to the other room. Feeling nervous, she clasped her trembling hands together and perched on the edge of the couch, her eyes fixed on the doorway.

When he entered, carrying both mugs of coffee, he came to stand before her, legs apart. Handing her one of the mugs, his eyes on her apprehensive face, he slowly sipped his own coffee. 'What exactly is it you want, Hilary? 'he asked quietly.

'Want?' she echoed stupidly.

'Yes, want. As in need, desire, as in what do you want, expect to happen now?'

'I don't know,' she said helplessly, which was a lie. She knew exactly what she wanted to happen now; she wanted him to hold her, tell her it was all right. Wrenching her gaze from his still face, she stared down into her cup. 'To go and see my parents,' she prevaricated.

'And then?'

'I don't know,' she whispered.

'Had enough of men for the time being?' he asked, his eyes still fixed on her unhappy face.

'Yes. No. Oh, Leo!' she exclaimed helplessly as she looked at him, a plea for understanding in her lovely eyes. 'I mean Matt. . .'

'Leo's fine.'

'Leo, then. I just don't know.' Staring up at him, she tried to read his own feelings in his eyes and couldn't. He looked and sounded so totally indifferent, as though all questions were hypothetical. 'Why didn't you tell me your real name?' she asked curiously.

'Because I didn't know if your mother had written mentioning me. She knew me as Matt and I didn't want to alert you to who I was until I'd found out what was going on. If you'd known at the beginning that I knew your parents you wouldn't have even given me the time of day. Would you?'

'I don't know,' she denied miserably. 'She didn't mention you.'

'No, so I gathered,' he said with dry mockery. Taking another mouthful of his coffee, he asked with apparent casualness, 'What did Ryan want?'

'You,' she told him bluntly. With an odd little grimace, she explained what Ryan had said. Expecting him to be amused, she was astonished when he swore, explicitly and very fluently, before draining the rest of his coffee in one swallow and thumping his cup on the mantelpiece. Leaning his arm along the wooden shelf, he stared moodily down into the fire.

'Leo?' she queried hesitantly. When he turned his head to look at her, his eyes flat and grey, she added in a little rush, 'I didn't feel anything for him. Nothing at all.'

'But then you don't feel anything for anyone else either, do you?' he asked indifferently. 'You're a coward, Hilary. An emotional coward.'

'Only because. . .' With a helpless little gesture, she put her mug on the floor. How could
she be anything else without knowing what he
wanted? She couldn't bear another rejection.

With an impatient sigh, he walked across to her
and pulled her to her feet. As he stared down into
her wide, startled eyes, he asked harshly, 'And
me, Hilary? What do you feel for me?'

Love, she wanted to shout, only his mirthless
smile cut the word off in the throat, and then
her breathing was cut off as well as he placed
one of her hands on the accelerated pulse beat-
ing in his neck.

'Desire? Need? Frustration? What?' he
demanded. 'You're twenty-seven years old, not
a child; are you going to spend the rest of your
life wrapped in a cocoon in case you get hurt?
Or are you going to spend it pretending that
every man who kisses you is Ryan?'

'No!' she exclaimed in shock. 'No! That was
said in anger and confusion because I didn't
want you to know how much you'd hurt me!'

'I didn't hurt you, dammit! You hurt yourself
with your over-active imagination!'

'I know that now,' she agreed unhappily, 'but
can't you understand why? I didn't know you.
It all seemed so logical that you knew Ryan, had
come over because of the land.' Staring at him,
at the strong face, her eyes drifted to his mouth,
the strong column of his throat and back to his
eyes. He still held her hand against his pulse
and she wanted to replace it with her mouth;

wanted to trail her fingers across his warm flesh, and the need to deny herself made her shake. 'Everything seemed to fit,' she continued shakily, 'I was afraid to trust my own judgement. I didn't know you,' she concluded lamely.

'You didn't know Ryan either, did you? Despite having lived with him for months.'

'No,' she agreed unhappily. But it's different this time, she wanted to tell him; this time I'm sure.

'You want me, though, don't you, Hilary? Physically, at any rate—I can see it in your eyes, feel it in the way your body is trembling. Your mind might fight against it, but your body is liquefying, melting, yearning,' he growled throatily, 'and it's very tempting to take what's offered and to hell with tomorrow.' When his eyes moved to her mouth, she swallowed drily, then took a long shuddering breath that locked somewhere in her lungs as he pushed the mac from her shoulders. 'So say it, Hilary, he commanded. 'Tell me you want me.'

Hardly able to get the words out, she breathed, 'I want you.'

'Then touch me,' he instructed. His voice was no more audible than her own had been, and his eyes had darkened to black. 'Touch me the way you touch Ryan.'

'No! I didn't touch Ryan!' she exclaimed. 'Oh, Leo, I didn't! Please believe me. He must have seen you through the window and he kissed me to punish me. Knowing you would see, misunderstand—as you have,' she finished miserably.

'Perhaps——'

'There's no perhaps about it!' she stormed. 'Either you believe me or you don't!'

'You talk too much.' Grabbing her hands, he placed them on his shirt-front. 'Undo the buttons.'

'No. I. . .'

'Hilary, undo the damned buttons!'

As she glared at him, almost hating him at that moment, he suddenly grinned, and her anger evaporated. With a shaky little breath she leaned her forehead against him. 'Oh, Leo.'

'Oh, Leo,' he mimicked.

Letting her breath out on a sigh, she looked up. 'It's not going to work, is it? All you want to do is punish me.'

'Yes,' he agreed quietly. 'I want to punish you—I also want to make love to you, so undo the buttons. Or I will.'

With a funny crooked smile he undid his own buttons, then gently pressed her face against his bared chest, his palms warm and hard against her head. 'Stop fighting me,' he murmured into her hair.

The feel of his warm flesh was too much to resist, and with a little groan she slid her arms round him. Pride was a puny thing compared to the feelings rioting inside her, and, with nerves stretched like piano wire, she began to caress his smooth back. She barely had time to assimilate the sudden rapid rise and fall of his chest before her head was wrenched back with a less than gentle hand and her mouth was captured by his. Not a gentle kiss, nor yet as punishing as the last one he had given her in her room, but it was urgent and demanding and was all the encouragement she needed.

Moving her arms to his neck, she clasped him as tight as she could and gave him back kiss for kiss. As she parted her mouth, her tongue parried the thrust of his and her breathing was agitated, almost desperate, as she fought to get closer to him. Standing on tiptoe, she arched her lower body to his scarcely needing the encouragement of his hand pressing against her spine. His belt buckle was digging into the soft skin of her stomach and she moved agitatedly, unconsciously provocative. Feeling his swift arousal, she dragged her mouth from his to bury it against his warm neck. She was crushed so tight against him that she could barely breathe, and as his own mouth moved to her ear, his tongue flicking erotically to trace the whorls, she moved her hands to his belt.

Muttering frustratedly as she struggled to undo it, in desperation she wriggled free of him to make it easier. Her hair a wild tangle around her flushed face, she looked up at him helplessly, and the expression in his eyes made her heart somersault crazily.

'Oh, Leo,' she whispered weakly, then closed

her eyes as one hand moved to touch her mouth. His thumb rubbed sensuously along the swollen lower lip while his other hand undid his belt buckle. Half lifting her lashes, she gazed into eyes that looked sleepy, at a mouth grown fuller from her urgent kisses.

'Now do it,' he said throatily as his eyes held hers captive.

Automatically obeying, she tugged the leather free, then delayed for a moment before releasing the hook on his trousers. 'Go on,' he husked.

Her eyes still fixed on his, her breath shuddering and jerking in her parted mouth, she completed the task. When he was completely naked, Hilary stood quietly before him, a well of excitement spreading from her groin to her breasts so that they tingled painfully.

He undressed her equally slowly, and she felt as though she were standing outside herself, watching almost with detachment as he exposed her breasts to his gaze and slowly lowered his head until his mouth could touch one rosy peak. Every nerve-ending felt exposed, her skin almost painful to the touch as she moved her hands across his warm skin, touched each muscle until it tensed, then slid her palms over his smooth back and buttocks.

Nothing else in the whole world seemed to matter except the sensation after sensation that flowed through her until touch was no longer enough. Sliding her hands round to his flat stomach, she lightly ran her fingers through the

hair arrowing down from his navel and he gave
a long shudder.

'Oh, Hilly,' he breathed. Folding her against
him, he gave a long sigh, then moved her back
so that he could look into her face. As she stared
into her bemused eyes, he slowly smiled, and in
that moment she would have committed murder
if he'd asked her to.

Smiling shakily back and in response to his
urging, she sank with him to the floor. Kneeling
across him, she joined her body to his with a
little gasp until he sat and touched his mouth to
hers. His body was tense, as was hers, yet they
didn't move, only their mouths touched and
they exchanged soft, drugging kisses that to
Hilary generated the most exciting sensations
she had ever experienced. The feel of him inside
her spread warmth through every part of her
until her body relaxed completely and gave itself
up to the purest pleasure. As they neared fulfilment, he rolled them slowly sideways until his
body was covering hers.

'Oh, Leo,' she sighed as she relaxed back
against the rug.

'Oh, Hilly,' he mimicked softly. 'Feel better
now?'

'Yes,' she agreed hesitantly, a small frown in
her eyes. He'd sounded almost taunting, yet as
she gazed up at him, and he smiled, she pushed
the doubts aside. Unable to help herself, she
touched her fingers lightly to his mouth, his
nose, cheeks, gaining enormous pleasure from

just touching him, watching him. 'Did you really watch movies of me?' she asked.

'Mm, and if we don't move I'm going to be burned all down one side.' With a hard swift kiss, he levered himself upright and Hilary stared unashamedly at his magnificent body, then grinned cheekily when he gave her a wry look. Extending a hand to her, she put her own reluctantly into it. She felt no desire to move at all.

'You're a very lovely lady,' he said huskily as he clasped her to him. 'Flushed from my love-making warm, soft and incredibly sexy.'

'Am I?' she whispered. 'Not rubbish?'

'No, not rubbish,' he denied. Threading his fingers through her tangled hair, he admitted, 'I was angry, and hurt, and, this morning, jealous as hell. Seeing him kissing you, I felt such a murderous rage that I wanted to storm in and beat him to a pulp. I thought I'd gone to all that trouble to lure you into my net, sort out the money, only to send you back into his arms. Did you really feel nothing?'

'Really,' she promised. 'He doesn't feel anything for me either. It must have been as I said; he saw you coming and deliberately kissed me. Quid pro quo,' she murmured. He'd also said Leo was a tycoon, only she didn't quite know how to ask him about that. In his present distrustful mood, he might imagine her to be a gold-digger on top of everything else. She wished she could think of something to say that would make him trust her, only after her stupid behaviour earlier she thought it might be a long time before he fully believed her. Maybe if she told him she was going out to Australia. Bending forward so that her nipples brushed his chest, which sent a delicious shiver through her, she rubbed her mouth against his. 'I gave in my notice yesterday,' she said softly against his lips, and she felt him stiffen.

'And?' he asked carefully.

'And I'm going out to Australia.' Moving back a fraction so that she could see his expression, she continued softly, 'You were right, I have been very stupid.'

'Yes. And Ryan means nothing to you?'

'No. Truly, Leo he means nothing.'

'All right.' He nodded, then, with a change of mood, asked, 'Want a bath?'

'Please.' Feeling a renewed surge of desire, she grinned. 'Together?'

'Of course together. What other way is there?'

When they had bathed in the old-fashioned bathroom, they climbed naked into the ancient four-poster bed that was surprisingly very comfortable.

'Modern mattress,' he told her before proceeding with the more pleasurable task of nibbling her ear.

Rolling over into his arms, she grazed her mouth over his chin, which felt slightly rough, and her body clung to his as though magnetised. 'Forgiven me?' she asked.

'I shouldn't,' he murmured. 'You accused me of being little better than a thief, a cheat, as though I'd masterminded it all just to hurt you. How the hell do you think that made me feel?'

'I said I was sorry,' she apologised meekly, 'and you did lie to me.'

'Well, yes, but that didn't mean you had to jump to all sorts of other conclusions.'

'Well, what else was I supposed to think? When Gwen said those things. . .'

'Gwen?' he exclaimed. 'What the hell has Gwen got to do with it?'

'Well, she said. . .' Trailing lamely off as she belatedly realised that Leo didn't know about the conversation she'd had with his sister, she bit her lip. If she explained it was going to get Gwen into trouble.

'No lies, Hilary,' he warned. 'What has Gwen got to do with this?'

Staring at him unhappily, she quickly explained, minimising Gwen's part as much as possible.

'So that's why,' he muttered faintly. 'I couldn't quite understand how you leapt from my knowing your parents to my being in cahoots with Ryan. So I guess I owe you an apology,' he said ruefully, 'although when you walked in through the kitchen door, all dressed up to the nines after being with Ryan, I wanted anything but to forgive you.' Glancing down at her, he asked with seeming casualness, 'Did she say anything else?'

'No, only that she didn't see much of you. . .' Suddenly remembering something the boy had said, she went pink, then white. His nephew had asked if she was the one his uncle was going to marry.

'What?' he asked.

Turning worried eyes on him, tempted to keep quiet, she sighed. If she didn't tell him he might accuse her of keeping something else from him and it might be best to know it all, mightn't it? Leo had never said he wanted a permanent arrangement, yet if he was going to marry someone else why get involved with her?

'Hilly,' he warned, 'what else?'

'Your nephew asked me if I was the one you were going to marry,' she blurted out as she averted her eyes from the probing intentness of his. 'And I just wondered. . .'

'Why I was bedding you if I was about to be married to someone else?' he asked softly. 'And it didn't occur to you that I might have been referring to you?'

'Of course it occurred to me! Only I didn't dare hope. . .' Her voice betraying her anxiety and doubt, she demanded, 'Were you?' He took such a long time to answer that she became convinced that he hadn't. 'It's all right,' she said hastily, 'I didn't—I mean I wasn't. . .'

'Expecting me to marry you? What did you

expect? That I was going to visit you each night? Take my pleasure then go home?'

Staring at him in confusion, she hauled herself upright in the bed and pushed the pillow behind her. 'I don't know,' she confessed. 'I didn't think beyond the moment. How could I know what you wanted? We've been so at odds the past few days. . .'

'That didn't change my feelings,' he denied softly, 'although I might have known you'd get the wrong end of the stick. Would you really have become my mistress?'

'Yes,' she said simply. 'It never occurred to me you'd want anything else—or at least,' she amended with a sheepish smile, 'I never dared hope you would want anything else. Apart from which, we barely know each other, know very little about each other.' Looking at him sideways, a delightfully confused smile on her face, she whispered, 'Do you really want to marry me?'

'Yes, I really want to marry you. Why do you find that so extraordinary? And, as for not knowing each other, we have the rest of our lives to find that out. We know we can turn each other on, we know that your body needs mine as mine needs yours. What more do we need, Hilary?' he asked gently.

'You aren't worried that there might be things about me that you won't like? Things that might irritate you?' she asked carefully. After Ryan, and the irritation he had often had with her, she was worried that Leo might become the same. 'Images on a home movie, second-hand knowledge of my personality, isn't knowing me, Leo. There might be all sorts of things about me. . .'

'Like?' he asked in amusement.

'Well, I don't know, do I?' she exclaimed, her brow creased in frantic thought. 'Maybe I leave the top off the toothpaste!'

'Well, do you?'

'No.'

'Then stop making up stupid excuses.' Folding his arms behind his head, he stared up at her, his eyes full of humour. 'There's some wine in the fridge. Want to go and get it?'

'Chauvinist,' she teased.

'You'd better believe it. Besides, I want to watch that delightful body sashaying naked across the floor.'

'Not only a chauvinist, but a voyeur to boot!' Climbing from the warm bed, she stood at the side for a moment to stare down at him. 'You really and truly want to marry me?' she asked softly.

'Yes,' he growled as he made a grab for her. 'Really and truly.'

Dodging out of the way, she said meekly, 'I'll go and get the wine.'

Walking with deliberate provocation across to the door, she struck a pose, then giggled when he threw the pillow at her.

Still laughing, feeling incredibly happy and

relaxed, she walked downstairs, although drinking wine in the middle of the day, and on an empty stomach, probably wasn't very wise. But then again, who wanted to be wise?

CHAPTER SEVEN

JUMPING the last two steps and turning into the hall, Hilary came face to face with Ryan. The smile wiped off her face, and quite forgetting that she was stark naked, she demanded shrilly, 'What the hell are you doing here?'

'Looking for your boyfriend, of course,' he drawled insultingly, 'What else would I be doing?'

'Then why not knock on the damned door?'

'Because he wouldn't have answered it, and I intend to have my money.' His face filled with sly mockery, he allowed his eyes to slide insultingly over her, and a sneer pulled at his mouth as he said softly, 'Maybe I was wrong to ditch you after all. I hope Verlander appreciates the skills I taught you.'

A hard light in her eyes, she drew back her arm and hit him as hard as she could across the face. Watching in satisfaction as his cheek turned scarlet, she enunciated icily, 'Now get out.' She didn't even flinch as he raised his fast as though to punch her.

'Don't so much as breathe on her,' Leo warned coldly as he descended the stairs behind them. 'Don't even look as though you're going to.'

Watching Ryan's face, she had to give him points for courage. She wouldn't have cared to face Leo in that mood.

Indicating with an arrogant lift of his chin that Hilary should go back upstairs, Leo planted himself squarely in front of her to shield from Ryan's gaze. Even naked, Leo didn't at all seem at a disadvantage, and, as she watched the two men, she finally and forever dispelled any lingering feeling she might have had for Ryan. Saw him clearly for what he was. Weak. His opportuniom, hio cheating, even hio charm, all stemmed from that one flaw of nature; weakness of character. Switching her eyes to Leo, she took in the strong bone-structure, the level grey eyes, and as she was about to turn and go back upstairs she saw Ryan's knee begin to lift as he reached out to grab Leo's arm.

Yelling a warning, which would have been far too late anyway, she watched in astonishment as Leo pivoted on one foot, and with a movement too fast for her to follow pinned Ryan up against the wall by his throat. Ryan's eyes seemed to bulge even as she watched, and she threw herself frantically towards them. Grabbing Leo's arm, she tried to drag him away.

'No!' she screamed. 'No, Leo, let him go!' She thought for a minute that he wasn't going to obey. He didn't even look as though he had heard. His face was a cold blank mask, only the eyes were alive as he stared at Ryan—and then, with one swift movement, he took his hand away so that Ryan crumpled to the floor.

'I told you to go upstairs,' Leo said coldly without looking at her. 'Now go.'

Glancing apprehensively from one to the other, she went; scrambled hastily upstairs, then wasted several minutes while she dithered uncertainly. Finally, grabbing the bedcover and wrapping it round herself, she crept back to the head of the stairs. She'd seen Leo angry, mocking, bleak, but she had never seen him look so coldly murderous, so devoid of any human feeling, and she shivered.

The two men were no longer at the bottom of the stairs, and, envisaging all sorts of dramas, including murder, she crept slowly down. Every time a stair creaked beneath her weight, she froze. Finally reaching the bottom, she peered theatrically round the end of the banisters, then crept stealthily along the hall towards the kitchen.

'If you're so concerned for his safety, hadn't you better get dressed and go after him?' Leo asked icily behind her.

Swinging round in surprise, she stared at him in astonishment. 'Go after him? Why on earth should I want to go after him?'

'Well, you seemed mightily concerned for his well-being.'

'Oh, don't be so ridiculous! That wasn't why I wanted you to let him go! How you do love to jump to conclusions——'

'*I* jump to conclusions,' he interrupted incredulously.

Ignoring that, she continued crossly, 'I wanted you to let him go because I didn't in the least fancy the idea of visiting you in jail! Holding hands through the bars is not my idea of fun!'

'Oh, you would have come to visit me, then?'

'Will you stop it? Of course I'd have come to visit you, you fool. You know how I feel about you, don't you?'

'Do I?' he asked on a sigh. Running a tired hand through his hair, he indicated her covering. 'Is that why you're creeping about looking like Pocahontas?'

'I was worried about you. I thought you might need some help—or something,' she finished lamely. Realising how ridiculous that sounded, she asked, 'So where is he?'

'Why? Did you want him?'

'No, I did not want him! And don't start that again. So, where is he?'

'Gone.'

Searching his eyes, not entirely sure she believed him, she walked round him to look into the lounge. Seeing no sign of him and deciding it would be a bit theatrical to go peering under the furniture, she swung back to find Leo lounging easily in the doorway, one shoulder against the door-frame, arms folded across his chest.

'Looking for bloodstains?' he queried mildly.

'No.' Staring at him, she suddenly gave a sheepish smile. 'Sorry. Did you hit him again?'

'Mind your own business.'

Walking up to him, the dignity she was trying to maintain spoiled when she caught her foot in the trailing bedspread and nearly fell over, she demanded, 'Hold out your hands.'

With an amused smile he did so, then turned them over to show her the backs. 'All right? No blood, no grazed knuckles.'

'You could have strangled him,' she pointed out.

'So I could, but I didn't.' Reaching out, he pulled her into his arms. 'But you can rest assured that he won't bother you again,' he added grimly.

'But what did you do?' she wailed frustratedly.

'Enough.'

Thoroughly exasperated by this lack of information when she wanted all the details, she shuffled round and went back into the lounge.

Following her, he gave a soft grunt of laughter at the sight of their clothes still scattered about the floor. 'Untidy pair, aren't we? Want a drink?'

'Please,' she said fervently. 'I think I need one.'

'Mm. I'll get the wine.'

When he had gone out, she gathered up their scattered clothes then folded them tidily and put them on a chair. After hitching her cover more firmly round her shoulders she made up the smouldering fire and sat on the pouffe. Chin on her fists, she stared into the glowing embers.

'If I promise to practise putting the cap on the toothpaste, will you marry me as soon as I can make arrangements?' Leo asked softly from behind her.

Turning to look up at him, Hilary absently took the glass he was holding out, then watched him walk across to sit on the sofa. He was still naked and seemed so relaxed in that state that she wondered if he often wandered around like that. In the privacy of his own home, at any rate.

'I go skinny-dipping too,' he murmured on a thread of laughter, obviously misunderstanding her stare. 'However, if it bothers you. . .' Picking up the cushion, he plonked it across his thighs. 'Better?' he asked mockingly.

'I didn't say it bothered me,' she denied softly as she sipped at her wine.

'Confucius he say, he who hesitates misses the boat.'

'Confucius didn't say any such thing.'

'Well, he would have done if he'd thought of it. Why so reluctant, Hilary? Want to check my credentials first?'

'No!' Seeing the teasing humour in his eyes, she grinned. 'I thought I'd already done that.'

With a laugh he tossed the cushion at her.

Fielding it with one hand, she sobered, and, putting her glass down on the fender, she hugged the cushion on her knees. 'It's not that

I'm reluctant,' she denied slowly, 'I just find it so incredible that you want to marry me.'

'Mm, it is a bit odd, I suppose,' he agreed, straight-faced. 'I mean, I'm so perfect, so sought after. . .'

Throwing the pillow back, her aim not nearly so good as his, she sighed.

'Why are you sitting so far away?' he asked softly.

'Because I can't think straight when I'm close to you. Do you live near to Mum and Mike?'

'Not far, a few hundred miles. It's only a few minutes by air,' he explained when she looked astonished. With a long sigh of his own, he rested his elbows on his knees and leant forward. 'You want explanations, is that it? OK. My name is Matthew Harleon Verlander, hence the Leo. I'm thirty-six years old and I seem to own half Australia.'

'You do what?' she asked faintly.

'Own half Australia,' he repeated blandly. 'Well, maybe that's a bit of an exaggeration; maybe only a quarter.'

'You said you were in property!' she accused.

'I am.'

'But not as an estate agent?'

'Not exactly.'

'What exactly?' she persisted. 'You buy and sell?'

'Er—no. Mostly I sort of own it,' he enlightened modestly.

'How much sort of?' she asked weakly as

vague memories of vast station properties stirred.

'Oh, a few thousand acres here and there. . .'

'Leo!'

'What?' he asked innocently.

'You *are* a tycoon, then?' she asked hesitantly. 'Ryan said you were.'

'Oh, good grief, why does his name have to pepper every conversation?' he asked irritably.

'It doesn't! But, seeing as you won't tell me anything, I have to use other sources. And I suppose all that Oxfam reject rubbish was just to throw me off the scent?'

'Oxfam rejects?' he exclaimed, sounding mortally offended. 'I'll have you know I choose my casual clothes with great care. And why should I try to throw you off the scent? I'm not ashamed of it, for goodness' sake!'

'But you are wealthy, aren't you? Very wealthy?'

'Well, there's no need to make it sound as though I'm a plague-carrier. And I suppose you are now going to spurt some rubbish about not possibly being able to marry someone who's wealthy?'

'No, I wasn't!' she denied. 'Marrying someone with money seems a splendid idea!' But it didn't, not really, and how wealthy was wealthy? she wondered, beginning to feel rather daunted. If he was some sort of local dignitary, or neighbourhood millionaire, how on earth would she fit into that sort of lifestyle? She was

a rep for a travel agents, for goodness' sake,
not a——

'Hilary,' he said softly, interrupting her
thoughts, 'come here.'

'No.'

'Hilary. . .' he warned. His voice was soft,
gentle, and he seemed relaxed, but the look in
his eyes was anything but.

Getting slowly to her feet, she went to stand
in front of him, the bedcover still held awkwardly round her. When he patted his knee,
she perched hesitantly.

Pulling her into his arms, he reassured gently,
'I love you, Hilary. Believe it, please. I think I've
always loved you, certainly it seems like it—and
you don't need to look so astonished; it was true
about the home movies, or partly, anyway. Your
mother talked about you constantly—she misses
you badly, you know. So does Mike. He spoke
about his beautiful Hilary with such pride, such
love, and, lying there in their spare room, with
nothing much to do, I thought about you too.
The laughing eyes, the ready smile, and, like a
schoolboy, I weaved fantasies around you. But
that's all they were then. Fantasies brought on
by boredom, or pain, or both. When I was finally
allowed up and I went back to my own home I
expected to forget you. Being reasonably
wealthy and not a total antidote to the opposite
sex,' he said with a wry grin, 'I knew there were
plenty of women to make me forget. Only I

couldn't. Whenever I took out Mary or Jane or——'

'Good God! It sounds like a damned harem!' she exclaimed waspishly.

'Oh, not quite,' he denied blandly. 'Anyway, all I could see were violet eyes and a wide smile, and, after a few weeks of being slowly driven to distraction by your lovely ghost following me around, I decided to come to England. I think I'd almost convinced myself that when I saw you I'd be cured. I contacted your parents for your address——'

'They didn't ask you?' she interrupted.

'No——'

'But you said——'

'I know what I said—that was pride talking,' he explained with a wry grin that successfully squashed her temper. 'I then wrote to Gwen, inviting myself to stay for a few weeks. I thought in my ignorance that Lorcomb would be just down the road from Norwich; when I discovered that it was an hour's drive I persuaded the colonel to rent me his house.'

'Just like that?' she asked in astonishment. 'You knocked on his door and asked him?'

'Sure. He was more than happy to oblige, especially when I explained why.'

'Of course,' she muttered, 'I'm sure it happens all the time.'

'Probably,' he agreed, his eyes full of laughter.

'So where did you tell him to go?'

'To my home, of course. I arranged his flight, contacted my manager to meet him, and——'

'You went to all that trouble just for me?' she demanded in bewildered astonishment. 'All that expense?'

'Don't you think you're worth it?' he asked softly.

Her eyes suddenly filling with tears, she shook her head. It seemed utterly incomprehensible.

'I would have done a great deal more, Hilary,' he told her seriously. 'I wanted you—and what I want I try very hard to get.'

Feeling suddenly shy, she looked down, and asked huskily, 'And, in return for a trip to Australia, the colonel told you all about me?'

'Mm. Not his fault,' he explained gently. 'I allowed him to think I already knew the bare bones of it, and he only discussed it then because he was fond of you, so don't go all stiff and prickly again.'

'And I suppose you only had to flash your smile at the women in the village to have them all falling over themselves to tell you more.'

'And that rankles, does it, Hilly?' he teased. 'That other women might find my smile charming?'

'Yes,' she admitted grudgingly.

'Good.' Shifting her into a more comfortable position, he continued, 'I was half prepared to dislike you on sight, you know. Quite convinced that meeting you would dispel the fantasy, and yet at the same time didn't want that to happen at all. What I wasn't prepared for was the jolt your appearance gave me. You looked so damned lost and unhappy, those beautiful eyes so full of shadows that, for the first time in my disreptuable life, I fell fathoms deep in love.'

'No. . .'

'Yes,' he insisted softly.

Looking hesitantly up, staring into his eyes, seeing the warmth and humour, the love, she felt weak. Recalling some of his taunts, the way he had treated her, she frowned. 'Did you expect me to know?'

'Yes. I thought women were always supposed to know. And do you honestly think that I normally allow females to wallop me across the face? Not once, but twice?' he asked humorously. 'If you hadn't known before, it must surely have occurred to you then, that it was a measure of my besottedness that I let you get away with it.'

'Besottedness?' she queried, laughing.

'Yes! I said once that I wanted to make love to you, not go to bed with you, and I seem to remember that I emphasised the point. What the hell was that but a declaration? It wasn't made lightly, Hilary.' With a warm, delighted smile for her confusion, he pulled her more warmly against him. 'Love doesn't have any reason to it, you know. It overrides all conception, all preconceived ideas of what you think you want or need. I saw you, and wham! All

those ideas of little blondes, or gorgeous red-
heads, flew out the window. I saw a haughty
little hedgehog and I was hooked. When we
made love that day in your room, and I experienced my own frailty, it shook me. To think
myself invincible, strong, all the weaknesses
ironed out, or subdued, it shook me rigid to
discover my total vulnerability where you were
concerned. And then I leaned up to look down
into your face, and saw the same vulnerability
echoed there, your eyes almost purple, dazed,
uncomprehending, and I knew then that I
couldn't let you go. I was going to explain then,
yet felt only a cowardly relief when we were
interrupted. I suppose I knew what your reaction would be, but thought in my arrogance that
if I presented you with a *fait accompli*, the sale of
the land, your money back, you'd be so over-
whelmed with gratitude that you'd immediately
fall into my arms.' His face serious, he pleaded
softly, 'Can't you pay me the same compliment,
Hilary? Be honest about your own feelings?'

'You know how I feel,' she began.

'No, I don't.' Holding her chin steady so that
he could stare into her eyes, he asked quietly,
'Could you love me?'

'Could?' she echoed in confusion.

'Yes, could. One day, do you think you could
love me?'

Staring back at him, aware of how still he was
holding himself, she exclaimed weakly, 'Oh,
Leo, *could* doesn't even enter into it. I love you

so much now, it hurts! Nothing you had done, or said, would have mattered if I hadn't. You must know that!' Yet why should he? She hadn't known herself until yesterday.

'I knew how I could make you feel,' he corrected, 'but there's a great deal of difference between bodily chemistry and love. Love has to grow, be nurtured; it's like a delicate orchid, it has to be watered, kept warm. . .'

'If you add pruned, Leo, I'll hit you again,' she threatened on a gurgle of laughter. 'And where, please, has the nurturing come in? I don't in the least recall being nurtured! I recall being shouted at! Derided! Insulted!'

'Well, that was a sort of nurturing,' he said with a funny little smile. 'I didn't know how else to shake you out of your melancholy—and I did so want Hilary back.'

Her eyes blurring again, she exclaimed shakily, 'Oh, Leo! I've been an awful pain, haven't I?'

'Not awful, never awful, just hurt and unhappy.'

'But not any more,' she insisted softly, 'and I do love you; I have no doubt about that. . .'

'Then what are you doubtful about? Living in Australia?'

'No, and if you were ordinary there wouldn't be a problem——'

'I am ordinary.'

'No, you aren't! No one who owns half of Australia can be ordinary! And marriage is more than loving and caring and wanting to do things together. It's existing side by side, sharing a sense of humour, a sense of the ridiculous! It's seeing me look like an old hag first thing in the morning and not minding! It's——'

'My dear girl, you could never in your life look like an old hag, and you seem to forget that so far I've never seen you at your best. Have I? You've been peevish, arrogant, downright rude on most occasions that we've met, so I'm hardly likely to be labouring under any illusions, am I?'

Giving a long sigh, she chewed on her lip for a moment as she wondered how to explain the other things that were bothering her. 'It isn't only that,' she confessed. 'I know less than nothing about you, and if you're important, which you must be if you're a, well, a tycoon, then I expect you entertain a lot—friends, business associates—which means that you'll need someone who'll be a credit to you—and I don't know if I can! I'm so ordinary, Leo!'

'Oh, will you stop being so ridiculous? My friends and associates aren't ogres, you know, they're ordinary blokes, as I am! I don't live any differently to anyone else! My life's an open book. . .'

'Yeah, the *Kama Sutra*,' she muttered.

With a shout of laughter that shook his solid frame, he hugged her hard. 'I wish,' he murmured, 'I'm not Superman, you know, and, flattered as I am by your assumptions, the truth is I'm usually too busy for socialising. Believe me, sweetheart, after a day working out with horses I'm——'

'Horses?' she exclaimed. 'You said you were in property!'

'I am,' he insisted firmly. 'I have a stud farm, and as I was saying I'm usually too shattered to do more than crawl into bed at the end of the day. Alone.'

Staring at him, at the strength, the energy that always seemed to radiate from him despite his easy, relaxed air, she didn't believe a word of it.

'Don't you like horses, Hilary?' he asked gently, the teasing light back in his eyes.

'Yes, I like horses,' she agreed lamely, then, unable to think of anything intelligent to say about them, asked something that seemed of far more importance. 'Have there been many women, Leo?'

'One or two. Does it bother you?'

'Yes,' she agreed, her voice roughening. 'The thought of beautiful women sharing your bed, touching you, tears me apart.'

'Then you'll understand how I feel about Ryan, won't you?' he asked grimly. 'Do you think I didn't hear what he said to you?'

'But that's different!' she exclaimed without thinking.

'Is it? Why?'

'Because, well, because—it wasn't like that! He didn't teach me anything! It wasn't ever like it was with you!'

'Wasn't it?' he insisted huskily.

'No; no, it wasn't.' Peeping at him sideways, curiously pleased that he might be jealous, she asked, 'Does it bother you? Really?'

'Yes,' he said simply, and his voice held such conviction that Hilary believed him. 'The thought of him touching you first, holding you in his arms—yes, if I let it, it would drive me insane.'

'Yet you didn't hit him. . .'

'Didn't I?'

Giving him a sharp look, she demanded, 'Did you?'

'What a very bloodthirsty girl you are!' Flicking a casual finger against her cheek, he admitted, 'Not then, no. There are other ways of dealing with rats like Ryan, ways that don't leave bruises—possibly a lawsuit,' he explained with a grin. Holding her eyes, he deliberately slid his finger down to push the covering aside.

Shivering with awareness, she grabbed his hand to still the movement. 'You never told me how you managed to get the money out of him,' she gasped.

With a long, theatrical sigh, he linked his fingers together round her waist. 'I did to him what he did to you. When I first found Ryan, which wasn't that difficult,' he explained drily, 'I offered him five thousand pounds for the land. . .'

'But he wouldn't accept that!' she exclaimed in astonishment.

'I know, and if you don't stop interrupting I won't tell you at all.'

Pulling a face, she clamped her lips together in a comical display of acceptance, although she was beginning to wonder if she actually wanted to know. His hand, which had insinuated itself beneath the cover, was sending her thoughts in an entirely different direction, and as his warm palm began rubbing gently across her back she totally lost track of what he was saying and had to desperately drag her mind back as he continued.

Ryan laughed in my face, which is what I expected. I then set about finding a genuine buyer, which was why I needed to know what sort of planning permission would be accepted by the council. If you have planning permission it's a hell of a lot easier to sell land. When I'd had confirmation that permission would be granted for one dwelling, no size specified, I toured round the estate agents, seeking a prospective purchaser.'

'And naturally found one,' she put in drily. Men like Leo would probably always achieve what they set out to do, including marrying her, she admitted ruefully. Snuggling more warmly against him, she encouraged, 'Go on.'

'As you so rightly pointed out, I found one. One who was willing to pay quite handsomely. I then, in true sneaky Aussie fashion, hired two young men who were willing to hold a fictitious conversation in a pub that Ryan frequented, which I must admit I thought rather a nice touch. Making sure that Ryan was already inside, they entered, sat near him, and began a general chat about land, A saying to B, in a casual roundabout fashion, that if he had any land going in Norfolk to unload it quickly because the councils were clamping down on building regulations and that land in future was to be used for agricultural purposes only.'

Laughing delightedly, she asked, 'And Ryan swallowed it?'

'Of course. Ryan is not very clever, you know. Malicious and greedy, but not very bright. That day he came into Frank Green's shop he was looking for me, and his seeing me with you nearly blew the whole thing. It took me quite a while to convince him that my being with you was because I was trying to persuade you to——'

'To persuade the colonel to ask his friends on the council to lift planning restrictions!'

'Clever girl. But not for real, I hasten to point out.' Giving her a narrow-eyed glance, he looked satisfied when she blushed. 'Anyway, seeing as that was the sort of thing Ryan himself would do, he believed me and I bought the land from him. I then sold it to the genuine buyer, paid you back. . .'

'And Ryan found out about it?'

'I made sure Ryan found out about it. Where was the point otherwise? I had to make sure he knew he'd been duped.'

'Which is why he was looking for you—
although how on earth he expected to persuade
you to pay up the difference I don't know!'

'No,' he agreed with a wicked smile.

With a little laugh, she said drily, 'Not at all
wise of him. And you did all that for me?'

'Well, I didn't do it for me!' he exclaimed.

'No,' she agreed softly. She still found it hard
to believe that someone would go to all that
trouble just for her.

'Believe it, Hilary,' he urged gently, and when
she smiled he whispered, 'Can we go back to
bed now?'

'Yes, please.'

'Mrs Hilary Verlander has a rather nice ring to
it, don't you think?' he added persuasively.

'Yes, it does.' Sliding her arms round his neck,
she pressed her nose to his.

'I can equip a workroom for you,' he offered
and, when she shook her head, added, 'I'll let
you ride my horses.'

'You haven't seen me ride,' she gurgled.

'I don't care. If there is any inducement I
haven't yet used, I'll find it and use it. I need
you, Hilary,' he added softly, his eyes intent on
hers. 'I don't know why you of all people make
my pulses race, my body respond; I only know
that it happens. I can't keep my damned hands
off you! Don't even want to! Maybe it's partly
due to that air of arrogant hauteur you have, but
I find it quite unbearably exciting to look at you

and know of the passion that's lurking under-
neath. That I can make that prim mouth curve
into a delightful smile. . .'

'I do not have a prim mouth!'

'Yes, you do, and I want it to say yes,' he
urged against her mouth.

'Yes,' she whispered, then smiled when he
went very still and drew back to stare at her.

'Yes?' he queried, almost in disbelief.

'Yes,' she confirmed. Bending forward, she
trailed her mouth delicately across the bridge of
his nose to his cheek, then down to hover
tantalisingly at the corner of his mouth. 'If the
thought of other women being able to do this,
to touch you, hold you, lie with you, brings on
the most awful pain inside, makes me feel sick
and ill, then I have no intention of letting you
out of my sight. Besides, as you so rightly
pointed out, I'm not getting any younger, and if
I want to have your children. . .' Yelping in
alarm as he tipped her sideways and moved
swiftly to trap her beneath him on the sofa, she
stared up at him in shock.

His face still, almost carved, the grey eyes
glittered with emotion. 'Children? Can I put in
an order now?' he asked huskily. 'Two little girls
who look like you? Oh, Hilly, how I love you!'
he exclaimed before she could answer him.
'Dear God, how I love you!'

Feeling heat burn behind her eyes, which
seem to spread with glorious slowness to her
body and limbs, she held him tight. 'I can't for

the life of me imagine why,' she whispered, 'but please don't stop, will you?'

'No.'

Calloway Corners

In September, Harlequin is proud to bring readers four
involving, romantic stories about the Calloway sisters,
set in Calloway Corners, Louisiana. Written by four of
Harlequin's most popular and award-winning authors,
you'll be enchanted by these sisters and the men
they love!

MARIAH by Sandra Canfield
JO by Tracy Hughes
TESS by Katherine Burton
EDEN by Penny Richards

As an added bonus, you can enter a sweepstakes contest
to win a trip to Calloway Corners, and meet all four
authors. Watch for details in all Calloway Corners books
in September.

Where do you find hot Texas nights, smooth Texas charm and dangerously sexy cowboys?

HEARTS AGAINST THE WIND

Strike it rich—Texas style!

Hank Travis could see himself in young Jeff Harris. The boy had oil in his blood, and wanderlust for the next big strike. There was nothing for him in Crystal Creek—except a certain marriage-minded Miss Beverly Townsend. And though Jeff seemed to have taken a shine to the former beauty queen, Hank wouldn't make book on Harris sticking around much longer!

CRYSTAL CREEK reverberates with the exciting rhythm of Texas. Each story features the rugged individuals who live and love in the Lone Star State. And each one ends with the same invitation...

Y'ALL COME BACK...REAL SOON!
**Don't miss *HEARTS AGAINST THE WIND* by Kathy Clark
Available in September wherever Harlequin books are sold.**

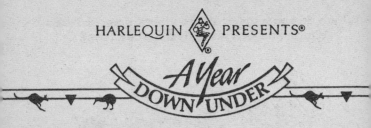

HARLEQUIN PRESENTS®

A Year DOWN UNDER

In 1993, Harlequin Presents celebrates the land down under. In September, let us take you to Sydney, Australia, in AND THEN CAME MORNING by Daphne Clair, Harlequin Presents #1586.

Amber Wynyard's career is fulfilling—she doesn't need a man to share her life. Joel Matheson agrees... Amber doesn't need just *any* man—she needs him. But can the disturbingly unconventional Australian break down her barriers? Will Amber let Joel in on the secret she's so long concealed?

Share the adventure—and the romance—of A Year Down Under!

Available this month in
A Year Down Under

THE STONE PRINCESS
by Robyn Donald
Harlequin Presents #1577
Available wherever Harlequin books are sold.

YDU-AG